DIG MY GRAVE DEEP

Peter Rabe worked for much of his life as a professor of psychology. Donald Westlake has written that "the understatement of violence" in Rabe's novels, "resulting from his modesty of character rather than modesty of experience," culminated in a method that "was refined...to a laconic hipness I could only admire from afar." Rabe published his unique brand of crime novels for twenty years, from 1955 to 1974. He lives in southern California.

DIG MY GRAVE DEEP

PETER RABE

Black Lizard Books

Berkeley • 1988

ISBN 0-88739-092-7
Library of Congress Catalog Card No. 87-72697

Manufactured in the United States of America

Dig My Grave Deep

Chapter One

AT SEVEN in the morning he turned over in bed and woke up. There was a cup of cold coffee on the nightstand next to his bed. He swung his legs to the floor, drank the coffee, and looked across the room with no show of interest. He could have lived there a week or a year—the room didn't tell—or maybe he didn't spend time there. He put the empty cup down and went to take a shower, after which he got dressed. At seven-thirty, when he opened the door to go out, the phone started ringing. It rang three times while he looked at it and moved his mouth to whistle. He walked out of the room and closed the door. The phone was still ringing when he went downstairs.

After a two-block walk he stopped at the glass and tile front with the big sign that said *United* and went in. There was a well-groomed girl behind the counter who smiled at him happily, because that's how she'd been trained.

"Daniel Port," he said to the girl. "Reservation on your noon flight to New York."

She got it ready and said, "Are you paying for it now?" and then she took his two large bills and gave him a little bit of change. When he walked out, the girl smiled at him the way she had been trained, but Port wasn't paying attention. He wondered what he should do between now and noon, and whether it wouldn't have been better to leave town some other way. It was eight in the morning and he felt hungry. When he found that there wasn't enough change in his pocket he decided to go back to his room for some money.

His door wasn't locked, but that wasn't unusual.

He closed the door and said, "Why don't you give up, Stoker?"

Stoker was short, and big around the middle. There was much loose skin in his face, like when a fat man goes on a sudden diet. The skin had the flush that comes from a bad heart. Stoker was sitting, and the other man stood next to his chair. He was the same size as Daniel Port, but very stringy, with no show of muscle. He kept his face in a tight scowl, except when it broke because of the tic under one eye.

"If it were up to Fries," said Stoker, and he gave the man next to him a look that was tired, "I wouldn't have come."

"Why did you?" said Port.

"You didn't answer," and Stoker looked at the phone.

"You got my answer. The last time you got my answer was yesterday."

"I remember."

They looked at each other for a moment, and then Daniel Port went to the closet and pulled out a suitcase. The rest of the closet was empty. He put the suitcase on the bed, opened it up, and took out some money. He closed the suitcase and looked back at Stoker, who had been watching without a word.

"You want to hear it again?" said Port.

"Better I didn't hear you the first time, Danny."

Daniel Port sat down on the bed and pulled out a cigarette and lit it. He couldn't say anything new because he had told Stoker all there was to be said several times before.

"Nobody walks out," said Fries. "Not even the fair-haired boy of the old man himself."

"Don't say that," said Stoker.

Fries reacted as if he had been insulted. It was a habit with him. He controlled himself and said, "Look at the closet, empty, and the suitcase there——"

"Don't call me old man," said Stoker. Then he turned to Daniel Port and looked him straight in the face. "About the rest, he's right, Danny. You don't walk out."

"I'm not walking out. I'm leaving."

"Nobody leaves," said Fries. "Did you ever hear of somebody leaving?"

"No—not before me." The way Port said it, without trying for any effect, Stoker and Fries both knew that he meant it. Stoker made his face go tired because he had to stay calm all the time. Only the flush in his skin started to waver.

Fries said, "You're so special? You any different from me? Don't forget it, Port, you're just a hood!"

"Was," said Port. "I was a hood."

Fries leaned forward a little, stretching his mouth to show how disgusted he was. "If I had my way, you sure as hell would be."

Daniel Port blew out smoke. He kept his mouth that way to give a tuneless whistle. He mashed out the cigarette in the tray next to the bed and when he was through and got up he was still whistling. The sound was mostly a hiss and he wasn't looking at anybody.

"I don't want it this way," said Stoker. "Don't listen to Fries right now. Danny, listen to me."

Port stopped the whistling noise and looked at Stoker, who looked pink in the face, but exhausted. Then he smiled at Port. "We still friends, Danny?"

"Sure," said Port. "You know that, Max."

"So listen to a friend, Danny. I don't want it the way Fries was saying."

"I know. But there it is. Either your way, or Fries's way. Right?"

"Right."

"How about my way?"

Then Stoker got up and went to the door. Fries opened it for him, but Stoker didn't go out yet.

"Don't leave, Daniel." He stepped out into the hall, then turned back. "I'm at the office all day. I'll be waiting. Come visit, like a friend." He walked down the hall, not wanting to talk any more.

Daniel Port closed the door behind them and went to the window. Stoker's car was in front. It was long and specially built, with a back door that was cut partway into the roof so that a man didn't have to stoop when he got in or out of the car. Stoker got into the back and Fries sat next to the driver. After they drove off, the street was empty. There wouldn't be anyone waiting for Port because Stoker didn't want it that way. He had said so. They had been friends and Stoker would wait for him, because that's the way Stoker wanted to run it. Fries was something else, but Fries wouldn't go against the old man.

Port remembered that he hadn't eaten. He left his room without bothering to lock it and went to the diner at the end of the street, where he ordered breakfast. He ordered the coffee first and let it get almost cold before he drank it. Then he walked back to his apartment. There were a few cars on the street, and a cruising taxi came toward Port, who could see the hackie's face, smiling and expectant. Port shook his head when the taxi stopped, but the hackie had the rear door open already. Then somebody stepped out of a doorway close by and came up fast. Port had never seen the man before, but when he was close Port hit the man under the heart. He could just see the man gag when Port suddenly felt that his head was coming off.

Chapter Two

THE SORE SPOT was on the back of his head and because he was lying against the car seat the movement gave him a lot of pain. He must have máde a sound, because they were all looking at him when he opened his eyes.

They were all suntanned; the one who had played the cabby, the wiry man next to the cabby, and the tall one in gray who sat with Port. The cabby turned around again to watch his driving, but the wiry one kept looking at Port over the back of the seat. He was chewing his lip, and there was a glimmery light in his eyes, hard and mean. Port remembered the man from the street.

The tall one next to Port said, "Sit still, Daniel." He didn't hold a gun in his hand, but Port sat back anyway and tried to relax. There was no point trying anything else.

The cab had left the residential streets, cut through midtown traffic, and headed out through the factory section. If this was a ride to the country, they weren't doing it right. If they wanted the river, or the warehouses, that was the other way. And they weren't going to any of Stoker's places, but perhaps that didn't make sense. It wouldn't make sense for Stoker to pick him up for another talk. The cab turned into the slums. They were getting close to Ward Nine, Stoker's own hot potato, but that wasn't going to help any now. Port knew the place well, all the streets and a lot of the people, but on this ride that wouldn't mean a thing. The man in front had his gun out now and the big one next to Port started to shift. When the cab stopped by the curb they were ready.

"Now you go out easy, Daniel," said the big one, "and mind you step where we say to step."

Port did as he was told, because the one with the gun was on the sidewalk already and his gun, back in the pocket now, was waiting for Port. The man stood with a

9

crouch, a careful bend of the back, as if he were holding a basket of eggs in front and afraid something might happen to them. The man was still hurting. Port stood on the sidewalk and watched the cabby and the tall one get out. They didn't hurry, but the one with the gun looked eager.

They had picked their place well. They could have shot him right there by the curb and not caused enough of a stir to worry about. The cabby was locking the car, because of the neighborhood, and Port waited, the gun spiking his back. There was cardboard on broken windows, and in some places there were scrawls making ugly figures on the sidewalk. Port thought that Ward Nine hadn't looked so ugly before; all the colors were lead-gray, as if the sky had a permanent overcast.

"In here," said the tall one, and the one with the gun took it up, poking the barrel into the soft flesh next to Port's spine. Port turned and walked to the basement door. There was a girl walking across the street now, watching the men go into the basement but not wondering about it. Port stumbled going down the steps. He waited while the cabby opened the door, and then he walked through. He thought he would like to see the street again, even the way it was, and, once more, the girl across the way.

The door banged and the cabby leaned against it. Port saw that much. And he made out a chair but nothing else. The room smelled wet.

"Sit." The tall one waved at the chair.

"Let him stand," said the one with the gun, and the gun came out of his pocket, butt end up. But the tall one reached out for the gun and pulled it free with hardly an effort. He dropped it into his pocket.

"We only talk, Kirby," and when Kirby made a quick move for his gun the tall one reached over and gave a push. Kirby stumbled across the room and slammed into the wall.

If Kirby hadn't been without the gun he wouldn't have stood there, but the tall one kept the gun in his pocket and turned to Port.

"He's sore on account of that poke you give him. We just came to talk."

Port felt the back of his head and said nothing.

"That's because you hit Kirby," said the tall one. "Else I wouldn't have clipped you."

Kirby came away from the wall and stood by the chair where Port was sitting. Port felt jumpy and it showed.

"Later," said the tall one. "Maybe later, Kirby. First we talk."

Kirby stepped away from the chair again, but just far enough not to rile the tall one. Port didn't relax. They were so slow about it, making no sense, that Port couldn't think straight. He had to look around the room to shake off the feeling of nowhere, but there was nothing to look at. Just the walls, one high window, and the door where the cabby was leaning. He was unwrapping a stick of gum.

Port had to say something.

"What's your name?" he said to the tall one.

"I'm George," said the tall one. "I'm here to tell you, Daniel, we want you shouldn't leave town."

"You working for Fries?"

"I don't know any Fries." George treated it like an interruption, very patient about it, and then got back to the subject. "Because you're leaving Stoker . . ."

"He sent you himself?"

George made an annoyed face, but he was still patient.

"I never seen Stoker," he said.

It meant nothing.

"You left him, didn't you?" and George stood in front of the chair, waiting for an answer.

Port said, "Why?"

"Because otherwise I got nothing to talk about."

Port said, "Yes, I left him." That's what he had wanted to do and if he hadn't said yes, George might have stopped talking too early.

"It's about the setup you got here in town," said George. "Stoker's bunch, where you come from, and Bellamy, the one that heads up the Reform party. You know who I mean."

Port knew what was coming. The relief he had felt hadn't lasted long, and he almost wished that George had been sent by Stoker. But that wouldn't have made any sense, Stoker pulling an act like this. Instead, he would wait in his office, just as he had said, and wait for Port to come back, because Stoker couldn't believe anything else.

But Bellamy would. He knew Port less and had more the temperament for a primitive stunt like this.

"Bellamy wants you," said George.

Stoker's loss would be Bellamy's gain. He would think like that. If you don't like Stoker, you got to like Bellamy. What else was there?

Port started to whistle and sat back in his chair. He waited till he felt that he wasn't going to lose his temper, that he could push it out of the way for a while. He said, "Tell me, George, then why any of this? Why this basement stunt?"

"Bellamy thought you'd be used to it."

"Or if you ain't," said Kirby, "then Bellamy figured it's time you knew what it's like."

"I'm surprised. Shocked and surprised," said Port. "After all, the Reform party in this town . . ."

"She's reforming," said Kirby.

"And then you had to come along and spoil it," said Port. He put his hands in his pockets to hunt for a cigarette, when Kirby swung with his fist. Port went blind with the water that shot into his eyes, because the punch had caught the bridge of his nose. A slow pain started to grow, leaving Port awake but feeling weak and alone. He even had room to think of the man who had hit him, what kind of man he must be, and real amazement went through Port's mind. Then the second punch knocked him out.

There was the bare wall again, then the high window, next to Kirby. This time Kirby was on the chair. And this time he had his gun. The tail end of a conversation went on with George saying something about wasting time and Kirby laughing that it was worth it, that there was nothing to worry about because it had only been the butt end of the gun, not the real McCoy.

"He's up," said the cabby at the door. He had a newspaper in his hand,, looking over it.

Kirby stood up and gave Port a kick. Then George was there too. He reached down, took Port by one hand, and pulled him off the floor. It felt worse than the kick. Port leaned against the wall and heard them talking at him.

"You're making a mistake, Daniel—"

"Make it again. Come on, sport, make it again—"

"He wants you to listen to sense. Bellamy says—"

"One way or the other, sport, have it any way you want—"

"Not the same deal like this Stoker. Bellamy wants you—"

"But the works, sport, whichever way—"

"Kirby," said Port, "which way is up?"

They both stopped. They watched Port straighten up, pushing away from the wall.

"Up? Up what?" said Kirby.

"Up yours," and Port swung from low down, catching Kirby under the nose so his head flipped back and then the whole man went over backward.

George caught him in his arms, because he was standing that way, and tossed the limp Kirby right back at Port. George would do something like that. Port had stepped clear and saw Kirby crash into the wall.

"About our talk," said Port. He hadn't moved again, watching George, and George didn't come any closer. As long as Port didn't make a wrong move, George wouldn't. That's where Kirby had been different, but now Kirby was out.

"Bellamy wants you to come over," said George, "and I'm here to give you the message."

"I left Stoker," said Port, "because I want out. I've had mine and now I want out."

"You can't leave."

"That's what Stoker said."

"Forget about Stoker. It's Bellamy now."

"I wouldn't do him any good."

"He wants you to come over. There's all kinds of dirt on Stoker, and you're the one who would know about it. Bellamy . . ."

"I told you, George, I'm through with the local dirt."

"You selling elsewhere?"

"No."

"You protecting Stoker?"

"You don't listen, do you?"

George shrugged, gave a short look at Kirby out on the floor, then turned back to Port.

"Bellamy wants the dirt."

"He can make his own."

George gave a short grin, which surprised Port, and said, "He mentioned that. To start with, he can make his own."

"Fine. That leaves me out."

"But you're in it." George laughed again. Then he changed back and was sober. "Think it over, boy. And don't try to leave town. Won't work."

George went over where Kirby was on the floor and

picked him up. He carried him to the door and gave him to the cabby. Then he came back.

"And keep your hands off Kirby," he said to Port. He hit under the heart and didn't wait to see Port sink to the floor. Then the door opened, and when Port looked again the door was still open but the men were gone.

Chapter Three

WHEN he left the building it was getting dark and the same overcast lay everywhere. Port gave himself time to rest and to look at the street. Then he saw the girl again.

he was coming the other way, on his side of the street, and she was wearing a different outfit of white nylon, buttoned down the front and very antiseptic-looking, like a nurse's uniform. But he was sure she wasn't a nurse. Her legs were bare and over one breast she wore a red carnation. Her skin was dark and her thick hair shiny black, making the red flower more vivid and the nylon more white. As she came closer she looked at him standing by the steps, but without special interest. She still didn't look away when she came past.

Port said, "Pardon me. You got the time?"

She said, "Close to six," and walked by without breaking her pace.

"Wait."

She stopped and looked back at him.

"I— You know, I saw you before, across the street."

"I know," she said. "I saw you go in here."

He walked up to her, smiling, but didn't know of anything else to say. He looked at her. He looked at her feet, then up, and stopped at her face. He didn't care what she thought. He smiled again and she must have misunderstood.

"No," she said, turned around and walked down the street without looking back.

After a moment Port turned the other way and walked steadily for a while, careful not to jar the aches in his body. By the time he had left the slums he was going faster. His mouth looked thinner, and hardly moved when he started to whistle.

The Lee building was closed when Port got there, but he rapped on the glass door and waited for the night man to show up. He came across the wide lobby, squinting to see the entrance. When he saw it was Port he got out his keys and unlocked the door.

"Evening, Mr. Port." He held the door open. "You lose your key, Mr. Port?"

"Is Stoker still in?"

"He's there. He said he wouldn't be leaving till nine or so, he and Mr. Fries. I think they . . ."

"Take me up, will you?"

"Sure, Mr. Port."

All the way up the night man wanted to say more but Port didn't encourage him. Port left the elevator on the tenth floor.

Stoker's door said *Civic Services, Inc.* The frosted glass showed a light. Port walked into the reception room, then through the big one with the desks and typewriters, and down the corridor with the doors to the private offices. One of them opened and Fries came out. He stopped short and stared.

"Where's Stoker?" said Port.

Fries didn't answer, but the frown came back to his face, and he turned and ran down the length of the corridor. He opened a door and before Port could get there he heard Fries talking to Stoker.

Port walked in. Stoker got up from behind his desk and Fries stood by, one hand working the back of a chair.

"What's the matter?" Port looked from one to the other.

For a moment nobody answered. The only change was the flushing color in Stoker's face. He leaned over his desk, looking straight at Port, and his breath was noisy.

"You son of a bitch!" he said.

Port stood for a moment and then took a step toward the desk.

"Sit down," said Fries. He hit the back legs of the chair on the floor and stood by, waiting for Port. "I said, sit."

Port saw Fries's hand come out of the pocket, holding a blackjack, and he walked up to the chair. He kicked it hard, making it fly into Fries's shins. Fries doubled over, sweating, and Port went up to the desk.

"Everybody nuts in this place? Since when does that creep go around telling me things?" he demanded.

Stoker sat down without answering. He looked over at Fries, who was straightening up painfully, and when Fries started for the desk Stoker said, "Go outside. Call Abe and his sidekick up here. They're down in the garage. And then wait outside."

"But if Port . . ." Fries started.

"He won't," said Stoker.

Fries left and Stoker waved at the chair.

"Go ahead, Port. Sit down."

Port sat down.

"I'm really interested," said Stoker. "So help me, I don't know why you came here."

"How could you. That's why I . . ."

"Shut up."

Port frowned but didn't say anything.

"Now, I admit I've been wrong before, like thinking you were a friend when you're nothing but a son of a bitch—"

"Stop calling me that," said Port.

"Wait till I'm through, Port. Just wait till I'm through."

Port let it go and sat back to listen. He knew that Stoker had to run himself out. He didn't get this way very often. He was long-winded only when he was too excited and wanted to calm down before finishing up.

"Come to think of it, now, I do know why you're back. What you did was just the beginning, and of course you and I know you got plenty more. So here you're back to let your old pal know . . ."

"Stoker, I don't know what you're talking about."

Stoker stared across the desk. He frowned and rubbed the loose skin under his face. "So help me," he said. "So help me if you don't sound like you meant it." Stoker put his right hand on top of the desk and put down his gun. Then he reached into a drawer, drew out a paper, and threw it on top of the desk. It came open, front up.

"Read it," said Stoker. "Unless you already know all about it."

Port picked it up.

STOKER MOB BLOCK SLUM CLEARANCE

The slum clearance project, long on the docket of our City Planning Board without receiving the urgent attention which it deserves, has long been stalled by machinations of the Stoker machine. Stoker controls Ward Nine, comprising the major area of substandard housing, and slum clearance and relocation of the Stoker machine vote victims would wipe out Ward Nine as a political tool. Is it therefore any wonder—and we give you proof positive, with names, dates, and reasons—why Boss Hoodlum Stoker and his Grand

Vizier Port have tried at any price, and to the detriment of
the unfortunates forced to dwell in the slums, and to the
total detriment of our city, have threatened and bribed
slum clearance into an all but dead stall. Planning Board
members Erzberg, Cummins, Utescu, threatened by Daniel
Port. Members Toms, and Vancoon, bribed with one hundred dollars in cash plus personal gifts and one hundred
and fifteen dollars in cash and personal gifts. The bribes
were arranged by Daniel Port and executed at his direction.
And all this in our city! Now it has long been the aim of
your Reform Party, etc., etc.

Port tossed the paper back on the desk and lit himself a
cigarette. When he looked up again Stoker sat waiting. Port
exhaled.

"This is news?"

"News! Now it's the truth, you jackass. It's been
printed!"

"Don't yell, Stoker. You can't afford . . ."

"If I drop dead I'm going to lay this thing out for you.
You walk out, you walk off with three guys we don't know,
you get lost all afternoon, next this mess of an Extra with
names, dates, and prices, and on top of that—and on top
of that you got the gall to come in here and . . ."

"Who saw me? Fries?"

"Somebody he sent."

"Did your bird dog . . ."

"Fries had the idea. Until now I didn't think it was
necessary to have a friend of mine shadowed."

"Did the bird dog also report that I got slugged?"

"That you made a good show of it."

"I could show you my wound," said Port. He mashed
his cigarette into an ashtray, which kept him from seeing
how Stoker meant to react. When Port looked up again
Stoker was leaning back in his chair, rigid with pain. He
tried to breathe carefully, and his face was suffused with
blood. Port jumped up, got the pills out of Stoker's vest
pocket, and dropped them on the man's tongue. They were
still lying there when Port put the glass of water up to the
mouth and poured.

After a while Stoker came around. He didn't look at
Port, but wiped the cold sweat off his face.

"That was a bad one," said Port.

"Closer." Stoker's voice was strained. "Each time closer
and closer."

Port frowned, then turned away. He went to the window and lit himself another cigarette.

"Danny," said Stoker.

Port turned.

"Danny. What can I believe?"

"You could believe me," said Port.

"You were walking out."

"I told you that months ago. I don't lie."

Stoker just nodded.

"And I'm still leaving."

"Then why did you come here?"

Port shrugged, getting impatient.

"I thought I had news for you."

"What was it?"

"It isn't news any more." He flipped one finger at the paper on top of the desk. "I got picked up and they told me they were going to spring something like this."

"Bellamy?"

"Not himself. He's too reformed for that."

"What did he want?"

"Me."

Stoker sat without talking, rubbing his chin with the back of his hand. Then he said, "You know why, don't you, Danny?"

"Because I was leaving."

"And you know why he sprang this dirt in the papers."

"There's nothing in that sheet that Bellamy didn't know months ago."

"True," said Stoker. He put both hands on the desk and leaned forward. "He timed it, Danny. He sprang it when it would hurt most—when you were leaving."

Port didn't answer. Instead he started to whistle. He sat down in the chair and got up again, and then Stoker went on.

"You still think you can walk out and nothing will happen?" Stoker sounded really tired now, and he kept plopping his hands together in a listless manner. "If I say, Danny, go ahead and pack up, you think that's enough? You know that isn't enough. You're taking too much with you. Sit down, Danny."

Port sat down. He wished he had left earlier, some other way, maybe, and he wished he had never told anyone about it. But it was too late now. And Stoker being his friend couldn't make any difference.

"Listen, Danny, how long we been together?"

"What do you want, Max?"

"Didn't I treat you right, Danny? You weren't so much, you know, when I picked you up after the war."

"I know. Lots of stuff but no application."

"But you learned. And now what are you doing? You're throwing it all down the drain. You don't make enough, maybe? Or you think this setup is too local or something?"

"I make enough, Max."

"So what is it?"

Port held his breath and looked out the window. It was dark outside. He thought that if Stoker didn't know by now, there was no use going into it again.

"Tell me again, Danny."

"I want out, that's all." Port tried to hold his temper, but it didn't work. "I want out because I learned all there was: there's a deal, and a deal to match that one, and the next day the same thing and the same faces and you spit at one guy and tip your hat to another, because one belongs here and the other one over there, and, hell, don't upset the organization whatever you do, because we all got to stick together so we don't get the shaft from some unexpected source. Right, Max? Hang together because it's too scary to hang alone. Well? Did I say something new? Something I didn't tell you before?"

"Nothing new." Stoker ran one hand over his face. "I knew this before you came along." He looked at the window and said, "That's why I'm here till I kick off."

The only sound was Stoker's careful breathing and Port's careful shifting of his feet. Then Port said, "Not for me."

It changed the mood in the room, as if Port didn't want to talk any more and had said all there was. Only Stoker didn't leave it that way.

"What else, Danny?"

"Nothing."

"It happened too sudden, your losing interest."

They both knew what Stoker was talking about, but Port didn't want to go into it. He was suddenly angry. He didn't say anything.

"When your kid brother got it is when you lost interest, isn't it?"

Port got up and went to the window, then back to the desk. He tried to talk very quietly.

"Bob got killed working for you. You sent him out to fix

up that policy trouble with Welman. For a talk—just to talk with Welman. Maybe that's all you thought it was going to be, but you also knew that there might be trouble. You knew Welman for a nut with a gun, and that my brother had more temper than brains. And you sent him out there."

"Blaming me—" Stoker started, but Port wasn't listening.

"I didn't want him to go! I didn't even want that kid hanging around you!"

Port took a breath and stared at the dark window.

"Blame you?" he said. "I don't know. I don't know whom to blame."

"Now you listen to me." Stoker put his elbows on the desk and rubbed both hands over his face. When he looked up again he nodded at Port. "You don't know whom to blame, but I know whom you're blaming. I'm going to . . ."

Port made an impatient gesture but Stoker didn't let him talk.

"I'm not done. I know you're going to ask what this has to do with your staying or leaving, so I'm telling you. Listen. I picked you up broke in New York, broke because you were wet-nursing that brother you had. The kid gets out of the army and falls in with bad companions and you to the rescue. He loses his roll. He gambles himself red, white and blue in the face and you stake him to a comeback." Stoker sat back and laughed. "All through the war, did you see him, did you nurse him along? No. He's in the Pacific and you in the ETO. Does he get along without you all that time? Sure he does; never a scratch. But you meet up in New York, you take care of him, and you both end up in the gutter. Right? Answer me!"

"Yeah. So what?"

"So I make a long story short and tell you I pick you up, I take you in, and from then on you started sailing. You and me, Danny, we got along fine because you got respect for a man who shows you what you don't know and you got it in you to learn."

"What's that got to do . . ."

"I said wait." Stoker lowered his voice. "And all this time you keep wet-nursing the kid brother along. Maybe you thought he was too dumb or maybe you thought I'd take advantage of him, but it comes out the same way: Dan Port, his brother's keeper."

"You're damn right I was my brother's keeper!"

"You don't have to yell, Dan. I know. Except for this."
Stoker paused to look up at Port's face. "Now I'll tell you
why you're quitting. Your kid brother's dead and it's your
fault."

Port didn't say anything because he knew Stoker was
right. He didn't say anything because he thought Stoker
was through.

"All through the war the kid gets along with no help
from you. Then you take him in hand and he dies."

"You said that!"

"To let you hear it. To let you hear that it sounds too
good to be true. So now here is the real stinger, why you
want to quit."

They stared at each other and then Stoker didn't let
Port wait any longer.

'The work you've been doing for me went along fine
and you never batted an eye. You could take it because
you were your brother's keeper. It made all the rest all
right, just like having a built-in excuse. Then Bob got
killed. You not only failed, Dan; you lost your excuse
for sticking around!"

Port was at the window and at the last words he
turned around fast, but when he saw Stoker he didn't talk
right away. After a while he talked very evenly.

"Now we both know. Now I leave," and he got up
without looking at Stoker.

"Dan."

Port stopped, turned around.

"Your brother is dead and you walk out." Stoker looked
up. "But I'm not dead—yet."

"It's got nothing to do with you, Max," Port said to
the wall.

"You're leaving when it's going to hurt most."

"You took care of your own before I came along."

"I wasn't this sick." He said it before he could stop
himself, and then he went on fast. "You're walking out with
that Reform thing riding the crest. After this dirt in the
paper, how long do you think I'm going to hold on to
Ward Nine? You know I need that ward, don't you? You
know if they tear down those slums, and spread the voters
all over the precincts the way it's been planned, you know
what'll happen to me, don't you, Dan?"

"I know."

"I lose the machine, I lose territory, I lose out with the setup from out of town. And you know what comes then?"

"You're a sick man, Max. They wouldn't drop you."

"That's why they would. Hard."

Neither of them said anything for a while and when Stoker talked again he was mumbling.

"If I tell you I need you, Dan—"

"I'm leaving, Max. I'm going to fix up that ward for you, and then I'm leaving."

Stoker looked down in his lap. "Better I didn't hear you, Dan. Just fix up that ward and don't talk."

Port walked to the door. He nodded his head without looking at Stoker and said, "All right, Max," and walked out.

Chapter Four

At eight in the morning Port was ready to go. When he went to the door he looked at the telephone but it didn't ring this time. Instead there was a knock on the door. Port stood back and said, "Come in."

He said, "Hi, Simon," and waved at the bald man to come in. Simon shook his head and grinned. "I brought something over, for a present. You going downstairs?"

Port said yes and they went down in the elevator.

"It's from the boss. He says I should bring it over with his compliments."

"Stoker must have had a good night."

"He arranged it yesterday. Called me up late and told me to bring it over by eight."

They got out of the elevator and walked through the lobby.

"You staying after all, huh?"

"Sure. So where's this present?"

"Right outside," said Simon, and when they got to the street, there was Fries.

Port stopped and gave Simon a disgusted look.

"What's the matter?" said Simon.

"You just ruined my day." Port turned to Fries, who came away from the curb where he had been waiting.

"Not him," said Simon. "He just come along for the . . ."

"Just one word with you, Port," Fries blinked the eye with the tic.

"Honest, Dan, I wouldn't play you a trick like that," said Simon. "I brought you the car. Stoker's present."

They all looked at the car by the curb, and Fries had to wait while Port went close to admire it. The car was a long convertible with a black nylon top and metallic gray body.

"It's a rare one, all right. No two-tone," said Port.

"And did you see the antennas?" Simon went to the rear. "One on each fender."

"For tuna fishing," said Port. "Fries, did you ever go tuna fishing?"

Fries wasn't in the mood. "Just one word," he said.

"Say it."

"I see you talked around the old man and you're back."

"That's right."

"Beat it, Simon," and Fries waited till Simon had walked out of earshot.

"And you want to tell me to take a powder."

"No. Nobody leaves," said Fries.

"I'm back. What more do you want?"

"Stay in your place. Just do your job and quit shining up to the old man."

"I should shine up to you. Right?"

But Fries didn't treat it as a joke.

"You can do that, if you think you know how. Might as well learn sooner than later."

Port stuck his hands in his pockets and grinned at Fries.

"Am I mistaken, or am I talking to the heir apparent?"

"I don't care what you call it . . ."

"But I might as well face the facts."

"That's right."

"So when the time comes, Fries, when Stoker doesn't make it with an attack, that's going to be my time?"

"That's going to be my time," said Fries. "That's when I take over."

"That's what I meant when I said . . ."

"I know what you meant. I'm correcting you."

"You sound like you're giving me a sentence. Am I gonna get killed?"

Fries made an impatient noise. "What's good for the organization is good enough for me. Just work like you have been and we're fine."

"And we might even be friends."

"I don't know what you're talking about," said Fries, and waved at Simon to come back.

They all nodded at each other and Simon nodded at the car too, and then Port got in behind the wheel. On his way down the street he passed Fries and Simon, who was walking a few steps behind, and the sight made the ward business that much more urgent to Port.

Most of the slum houses were frame, but a few were brownstone, and the one in the best repair had a clean, sandblasted front with a small sign that said *Social Club*. The inside was mostly new. There was an addition which

held a gym, a foyer with a cloakroom, and past some
columns varnished dark brown was a bar, the room with
the easy chairs, and a bare place with a stage and some
folding chairs stacked by the walls. Upstairs there were
more rooms.

The whole place had been paid for and built for Boss
Stoker. He had never been there, which made little difference as long as the place was for Stoker.

Daniel Port left his car in the front by the No Parking
sign and headed for the stairs. Before he got to them
he turned back, locked both doors of the car, and then
went into the club.

Downstairs looked empty. In the room with the easy
chairs Port found two men sitting by the fireplace. They
had a small volley ball and kept tossing it back and forth.
Port said, "Is Lantek in?" and the men looked around
at him.

"Should be," said one of them. They kept tossing the
ball. Port went upstairs without seeing anyone else, until
he came to the back corridor. The man at one of the doors
paid no attention to Port.

"You seen Lantek?" said Port.

The man looked up and nodded. Then he leaned back
against the wall and looked at his magazine. Port tried
again.

"Where is he?"

"Who wants to know?"

Port had never seen the man before. He was slight and
dark, and Port guessed what the man lacked in strength
he might well make up in speed.

"You new here?" said Port.

"Yes. Perhaps a month."

With Lantek at the club, things could mostly be run by
phone, and Port hadn't been there in over a month.

"All right. Where's Lantek?"

"He's busy. Come back in half an hour."

"You're new here," said Port. "You don't know who I
am. Just tell me where Lantek is."

"Who are you?"

"Dan Port."

The man closed his magazine quickly and looked attentive. "I'm sorry," he said. "I didn't know who you
were. If I can do anything . . ."

"You can tell me where Lantek is."

The man was uncomfortable. He wanted to please, but. he couldn't.

"He told me—he said not before half an hour. I'm new here, and maybe you better . . ."

"He's in there?" and Port looked at the door, because the new man had edged himself in front of it.

"He is, Mr. Port, but he said nobody, or nothing, for half an hour."

"You're eager," said Port. "I bet Lantek likes that."

"I hope so," said the man.

"Don't be so eager it makes you scared. Open that door."

The new man stepped aside and let Port go in.

The room had a table, some chairs, and a couch. They were all by the couch, backs to the door, and they didn't notice Port right away. Only the girl did, because she was facing his way. She got off the couch and looked sullen. She said, "He's extra. He's not part of the deal."

She wore shoes and a blouse—and nothing else.

Port closed the door and they all looked at him. There were Lantek and several others.

"Jeez," said Port. "It's only ten in the morning!"

The girl walked up to Port and stopped with her hands on her hips. She said, "Don't act like I asked you to take a drink before noon. All I said was . . ."

"Put your clothes on," said Port.

Lantek stepped up, a big man with his hair cut down to a stiff stubble and a jaw like a trap. He smiled at Port and shrugged one shoulder.

"Hell, Danny—you want in on it?"

"Not if you don't raise the ante," said the girl. One of the seven others was trying to shush her but she pushed him aside and got louder. "When I make a deal—" she started, but Port interrupted.

"Lady, there's no deal. Put your clothes on and go."

They all started talking together and they all had the same thing in mind. Lantek couldn't keep them quiet and Port didn't try. He waited a while longer till they were all looking at him.

"Put your clothes on," he said to the girl.

She put on the skirt and a jacket and buttoned up, not

looking happy about it. "I didn't get paid yet," she said.

"For what?" said one of the men, and another voice, "Nothing happened. Why should . . ."

"I come up here!" said the girl, angry now. "What about wasting my time and—the indignity!"

"Get out," said Lantek.

His voice made her jump and she started for the door.

"She gets paid half," said Port. "For her time—and the indignity."

He lit a cigarette and waited while the girl collected the half-fee and then left the room. Then the men stood in the room, without talking, waiting for Port.

"Which one of you guys handles the phone in this place?"

One man raised his hand, but didn't say anything. Then Port wanted to know who did the soliciting, who made the rounds on the charity cases, which one ran the errands, and who kept the books. He nodded each time a man raised his hand, and when he was finished he left a moment of silence, making them all hope he was through. Then he dismissed them.

They were out of the room in short order, leaving only Port and Lantek, who was rubbing one hand through his hair and looking back and forth between Port and the window. Port looked at him briefly. He mumbled, "Jeez. At ten in the morning," and opened the door. The new man was still standing there. "Bring him along," said Port. He went into a room fixed like an office, sat down at the desk, and waited for Lantek and the new one to come in. Lantek sat down by the desk, but the new man stood.

"I never asked you your name," said Port.

"I'm Ramon. Calvin Ramon."

"You say Calvin?"

"He's Mexican," said Lantek, as if that explained it. "Or Spanish."

"My parents were," said Ramon. "I was born here. I mean in Los Angeles. And my parents had it in their minds —they always said, 'A new country, a new name. Make a break with the past.' You know what I mean."

Port said, "Oh," and crossed his legs. He turned to Lantek. "I need a man to head up a team collecting signatures. Can you spare him?" He nodded at the new man.

"Sure," said Lantek. "But he's new. I can get you Cholly—or how about Tim, if it's really important. I been keeping my eye on Tim for a while now, and the way I see it . . ."

"Look," Port sounded resigned. "We fix men up with jobs all the time. We do it all over the city and with some of the county jobs." Then Port sat up, talking more clearly, "But we don't horse around like that with jobs in the organization! Try to remember that." He looked back at the new man.

"Here's what it is, Ramon." He handed Ramon a typed sheet of paper. "It's a questionnaire. Have that mimeographed and then get twenty men from Lantek to make the rounds. It says yes and no, behind the answers. They should all be marked. On the bottom I want signatures. Real, original signatures. Okay with you, Lantek?"

"Sure, Danny, sure."

"Hand them out tonight, starting at six, and have them ready for me here at nine in the morning. Okay, Ramon?"

"Sure thing, Danny. I'll start now."

"Have the mimeograph done by Schuster, on Lane Street and Scranton. Know where that is?"

Ramon was so anxious to say yes, he started to stutter. He didn't know where the place was.

"I'm driving by there," said Port. "Come along."

Port told Lantek to line up twenty men for six sharp, and left with Ramon. When they got to Port's car Ramon hadn't stopped talking once. He apologized for being new, he was grateful for being given the chance, he would do all he could, and when they got to the car he started admiring that. "And back here," he said, walking around to the trunk, "what lines, what antennas! You know something, Dan? I've lived in California. Did you ever see those boats they have, those boats they rig up for tuna fishing? These antennas here . . ."

"Is that so?" said Port. Then he offered Ramon a cigarette. "Come on across the street. I'll buy you a coffee."

They went into the short-order place with the grocery counter in front and sat down near the grill. Then they waited for someone to show.

"You know why I picked you?" said Port.

Ramon shook his head.

"Because you're eager."

"I am, Dan. I think this town has opportunities. What I mean is, I can really do something for this—in this club, because when I have half a chance . . ."

"I know," said Port. "I know what you got in mind."

"With half a chance . . ."

"Sure, Ramon. I use you and you try the same with me and we both win. That what you mean?"

"I don't really mean . . ."

"Ramon, listen. I'm in a hurry, and you're eager. That's why I picked you, and you like it for your own reasons. Okay? Don't bring it up again."

Ramon didn't answer, just nodded his head.

"Now listen close," said Port. "Here's the rest of the deal."

"About the mimeographing?"

"After the mimeographing. This is something else."

Ramon got very attentive but Port didn't say anything else. He watched the waitress come in from the back, seeing the red carnation before he had seen her face. She put a soup pot on the grill. When she recognized Port her face stayed as bland as he remembered it from the street. Then she smiled, and it was an easy smile which changed her face in a beautiful way. "Nino," she said. "You didn't come home last night." Then she got two cups of coffee without asking.

"I'm five years older than she is," said Ramon, "and she still calls me Nino."

"Yeah," said Port. He picked up his coffee, burned his mouth, because he wasn't used to drinking it hot.

"Meet my sister," said Ramon, and to her, "this is Daniel Port."

She smiled again, but less than before, and said, "How are you? You look better today."

"Thank you," said Port. "You look the same. It's hard improving on you."

She raised her eyebrows at him, giving a half-smile, and went to the grill to set the soup into the steam table.

"You know each other?" asked Ramon.

"No," she said. "We just met on the street."

"I asked her the time," said Port.

Ramon nodded and drank his coffee. He watched his sister and he tried watching Port, but he couldn't tell a thing. If they knew each other they didn't show a thing. It might be nice if they did. There would be no harm done, if Port would show interest.

"Finish up and we'll go," said Port. He put thirty cents on the counter and got up.

"You were going to tell me something else," said Ramon. "Some other deal you had in mind."

Port waved at Ramon's sister and said, "See you again." She smiled and nodded. You could make of it what you wanted.

Outside, Port crossed the street to his car and got behind the wheel. Ramon sat next to him. Port started the car.

"You never told me her name," he said. "I'm sure it can't be anything like Dolores or Carmen."

"Her name is Shelly." Ramon looked out the window. "You like Shelly?"

"It's better than Calvin," said Port.

Chapter Five

RAMON came back to the club at eight the next morning. He pushed the front door open with one shoulder, because he was carrying the questionnaires with both hands. In the front hall he put the stack on the counter of the cloak room and took a deep breath. He felt like sitting down; he wanted a cup of hot coffee and afterwards some sleep. The job had been more work than he'd figured. It had taken all night. There were only three questions with only a "yes" or "no" answer, but it had taken all night to tally them up. Shelly had come into the kitchen twice and offered to help him. He had told her to go back to bed, the job was too important.

Ramon stood behind the counter and stacked the sheets. Then he went to the bar and found a carton with empty whisky bottles. He put the bottles on the floor, took the carton and put the stacked sheets inside it.

At eight-thirty Lantek came in. He nodded at Ramon and came over to look into the box. The top sheet had the totals on it.

"What you got here?"

"The questionnaires. You remember, Dan told me•. . ."

"This here," and Lantek took up the sheet with the totals.

"I added the whole thing up. I was sure we'd need the whole thing tallied, so I did it last night. Don't you think . . ."

Lantek looked ill-humored and put the sheet back.

"You're wasting your time," he said. "Dan don't impress."

"We need the tallies, don't we?"

Lantek looked up at the tone but didn't say anything. The whole thing was done, anyway. "You're done," he said, and picked up the box.

"Leave it. I'll give it to him. I'm supposed to wait for him anyway."

Lantek put down the box. "You're done, I said."

They looked at each other for a moment.

"Out, Ramon. And don't come back."

Ramon felt suddenly weak, with a filminess getting into his vision. His effort to get back his strength made the sweat come out on his forehead. But then he couldn't talk.

"Don't look at me," said Lantek. "I get my orders, same as you, straight from Port."

He picked up the box with the stack of papers inside and went to the stairs. Before going up he turned and called back. "You waiting for me to throw you out?" He stood at the bottom step, watching, till Ramon had gone out of the door.

At first he was not going anywhere, just walking away, but when he got down to the street he had to stop because the tension would not let him walk any further. To leave now would make the break physically final. From one day to the next—and all night, working to get it done for the next big day—Shelly sleeping in the next room, plans and thoughts about what he would do with—for—Shelly. He was going to throw her at him. His own sister. He was going to get her messed up with that Port bastard who had it in his hands to make or to break him.

Ramon sat down on the steps of the club and scraped his nails over his scalp. His throat pained, as if he had been screaming. He raked his nails through his hair, made two fists and held on. Whom would he kill first? Port? Of course Port, and then that swinehead back in the club. And there were a few more that might get in his way and the thing would be . . . But first back to Port.

Ramon heard footsteps on the pavement and sat up immediately. He coughed hard, distorting his face. He did this without thought, but it served to blank out what he had been doing, as if it was necessary to blank it out or else it might show. Whoever was walking on the street would see Ramon on the steps, coughing.

Across the street a boy was walking by and he looked at Ramon only because he was coughing.

Now that Ramon was not thinking about the murder any more he felt lost and aimless. Ramon did not feel that he wanted to see anyone he might know, because his feelings were out of hand, confused and painful. Of course with Port it would be different—there would be the sharp, clear, incisive thing. When Ramon turned to cross the street the car slid up and cut off his view. The two antennas dipped and weaved over the massive hulk of the car. If heraldic standards had flown from the antennas it would not have surprised Ramon.

Port looked at Ramon over the top of the car while he slammed the door shut.

"Morning. You been inside?"

Ramon stared at Port, waiting for his rage to come to him.

"Hey—Calvin!"

Ramon started chewing his lip, but no rage came to his aid, not even insults. Port came around the car, one hand in his pocket. He stopped with one foot on the curb, and looked at Ramon. Port was so casual, Ramon thought for a moment he could hit the man now.

"Come along," said Port. "I'll buy you some coffee."

Then Ramon ran after him and started to talk before he even caught up. "Why? Why did you do it? You threw me out without even a chance for me to make good, to do anything. I'm a member for two weeks, after it took me maybe three months—ever since we moved into the neighborhood. And you don't even—"

He stopped when Port turned to look at him at the door to the shop. Ramon burst out, finally angry.

"Did you tell that swinehead to throw me out? Did you?"

"Sure I did," said Port, and held the door open for Ramon.

Ramon looked inside and remembered that Shelly would not be there, not until later. He went in and sat down at the counter.

"Two coffees," said Port to the man at the grill. Then he looked at Ramon. "Now shut up and listen."

Ramon sat still, his mouth open.

"You wormed your way into the club. You're in for two weeks, and you get thrown out. We don't want you. That's what Lantek knows, that's what anybody knows who cares to ask about it." Port stopped to blow on his coffee. "I got a job for you and for that job you got to be thrown out of the club."

Ramon burned his mouth on the coffee.

"Now here's the deal. Let me know if you want it."

Ramon had a sensation of quivering and was afraid it

might show. He sucked in his breath, he smiled with mouth wide and stiff.

"Sure, Dan. Anything. But why didn't you tell me? Why send Lantek—and me not knowing a thing, Dan. I thought I was going nuts!"

Port looked at his coffee and blew on it.

"Don't get so eager it makes you scared, Ramon. I told you once."

"You can talk. You're on top, and nothing can . . ."

"You had a bad morning?" Port paused. "When you're in, Ramon, this happens all the time."

Port drank coffee and didn't say any more for a while. He poured water into the coffee and drank it that way. Ramon sat and waited. He thought about what he had heard, and didn't believe a word of it. After a while he said, "You have a job for me?"

"As a gardener."

"You mean—in a garden?"

"Go to the Apex Employment Bureau. They know you're coming. They got a request for a gardener and I want you to apply for the job. You'll be the only applicant, so you shouldn't have any trouble. Sam White at the agency will show you a sheet with dates and references. Learn it by heart, because that's your background. You've been a gardener most of your life." Ramon listened for more.

"After you try for the job go home and wait for me there. Where do you live?"

Ramon told him.

"I'll be over late. If you have the job, I'll tell you the rest." Port got up, paid for the coffee. "And keep away from the club. You're out, and you don't like it."

Ramon nodded and watched Port walk out the door. Ramon felt he should be elated, now that everything was again well in hand; except, as he found it, nothing seemed to be in his own hands.

Chapter Six

PORT pulled the car into a space marked *Reserved for Officials,* and walked into the Municipal Building carrying the whisky carton with the questionnaires under his arm. Inside he said hello to the guard at the information desk and walked to the elevator. The old man who ran it said, "Nice seeing you, Danny," and tried to carry the box into the elevator for him. Port thanked him and held on to it himself. He said, "Is McFarlane in?"

"He's always in," said the old man.

"That figures," said Port. "It takes double time, playing both ends against the middle."

"Why you keep dealing with him, Danny, knowing he isn't straight?"

"If he were straight, Pop, you think he'd be dealing with me?"

The old man pulled his head into his shoulders and didn't answer. He let Port out on the third floor and watched him go through the door where it said *City Solicitor.*

The city solicitor wasn't in until Port told the girl who he was. "Mr. McFarlane will see you," she said. "Since you told me so." Port predicted for her a fine future with the fine attitude she was displaying, but advised that it would be better if she got married instead. She said that was her plan, except she was right now beholden to Mr. McFarlane, who would be unable to keep his composure if ten times a day he couldn't watch the way her back curved when she sits on her typist's chair. She swiveled toward the half-open door of the inner office and said, "Did you want me, Mr. McFarlane?"

There was a severe *harrump* and the door opened all the way. McFarlane came out with strides that were meant to suggest how busy he was.

"Hello, Port. All right, Miss Trent, are you finished with—"

"Yes, Mr. McFarlane." She handed a folder to him.

McFarlane had twitchy eyebrows which detracted from the fact that he rarely looked a person straight in the face. Miss Trent turned her back, curved it beautifully, and started to type. McFarlane's eyebrows stopped jumping, but then he remembered Port. "Come along, Dan," he said, and took hasty steps into his office.

Port stood by the window and watched McFarlane settle down behind his desk. After a while Port said, "About that slum deal, McFarlane. What's your thought?"

"Hardly my problem." He looked at his fingernails and then up at Port. "Why this visit? Come to the point."

Port folded his arms and sat down on the window sill. "Where is the recommendation to raze the slum district?"

"It's left City Planning. You know that."

Port smiled. "It left the commission a year ago. What I mean is, how hard is Bellamy pushing to get it before City Council?"

"You read the paper, didn't you? Then you know how hard he's pushing." McFarlane made a nervous squint while he lit a cigarette. "You're wasting time, Port. My time, at any rate."

Port's smile got wider, and then he laughed. "It's a fact you aren't wasting any time, McFarlane. A day hasn't passed since Bellamy's move, and already you hate to be seen with me. You sure Stoker will lose his ward?"

McFarlane puffed hard on his cigarette. He almost looked at Port, but his eyes wandered off again.

"So far, the slum clearance thing is only a resolution," said Port. "It's before the council, or will be, but it hasn't been passed upon yet. They haven't even debated."

"You're whistling in the dark," said McFarlane.

"I'm just trying to give you courage, Counsellor."

McFarlane got up to reach for papers.

"I'm busy, Port. I'm very busy. I'm due at a hearing in half an hour, and I've got to . . ."

"Then you got half an hour. Tell me, McFarlane, did you make a ruling on that recommendation? City codes, and so forth?"

"There was no need for a ruling. You know that this slum clearance thing is clean all the way through."

Port came away from the window and sat down by the desk.

"The council can't vote the recommendation for clearing the area into special ordinance unless your office gives a legal ruling."

"Look, Port. That thing has come through my office maybe a dozen times, and you know it. It's routine when a resolution is as pure-white as this."

"Let's say you were asked, McFarlane. Let's say you were asked if that slum clearance project didn't violate city statutes. Would you know?"

"Of course I'd know! Who do you think is responsible for the legality . . ."

"You are. And I'm asking."

"It's clean! All the way through!"

"Don't act like it frightens you, McFarlane."

McFarlane controlled himself and hunched over the desk. His eyebrows stopped jumping, stayed way up on his forehead, and he talked with theatrical patience.

"The old lodgings don't meet architectural codes; the proposed new ones do. The old lodgings don't meet health department ordinances; the new ones do. The old lodgings don't meet zoning laws; the new ones do. The old lodgings . . ."

"So you have no thoughts on the subject, is that right?"

McFarlane sat up again. "What do you mean?" he asked.

"Here's what I want you to do," said Port. "Make a ruling on the assessment for utilities."

McFarlane waited.

"You and I know, McFarlane, that the utility companies aren't willing to pay more than fifty per cent of the cost for new installations in the homes for resettlement."

"Whatever you have in mind, you and I know that the city will pay the difference."

"By special assessment. And you, Counsellor, are the one who decides whether the special assessment is allowable under existing city ordinances."

"It is. And now, Port, if you will excuse . . ."

"It isn't."

McFarlane sat down again.

"The assessed money comes from taxes. Taxes are paid by the people. This assessment to pay for utilities benefits only some of the people. Under its statutes this city—any city, McFarlane—is not authorized to apply tax funds for the benefit of a special group." Port looked inquisitive. "How's it sound, Counsellor?"

This time McFarlane looked straight *at* Port, but he didn't say anything.

"They can't tear down the slums," said Port, "because the slum dwellers have no place to move. They got no place to move because the projected settlements won't have any utilities. They won't have any utilities, because the companies only pay fifty per cent of the new installations—and the city won't pay the rest. The city can't. Violation of statutes."

"That's my ruling?" said McFarlane.

"That's your ruling."

"What if I don't?"

"I'll tell Councilman Epp to bring it up at debate. Then the question will be why in hell you didn't look into that point. Neglect of office, McFarlane." Port shook his head.

McFarlane got up, stacked some folders together, and put them under his arm. He put out the cigarette that was smoking itself in the ashtray, and went out the door, Port following him.

"How do you want me to submit it, at debate?"

"Leave the grandstand plays to Reform. Just submit it in writing to the council committee that'll bring úp the debate. A quiet demise."

"Whatever you like," said McFarlane. He watched Port pick up his whisky carton. "I don't know how quiet it will be. Sump is chairman of that committee. You know Sump."

"I didn't mean to keep this thing buried. Just dignified."

"Sump will take care of that, too," said McFarlane.

Port laughed. "He after you now?"

"I told you I have this hearing." McFarlane looked at his watch. "And I'm late."

Port laughed and opened the door. "I'll go with you. Then you can blame it on me."

When they went through the office in front Port stopped where Miss Trent was typing and put his carton on top of the desk.

"May I leave this with you?"

She looked up and smiled straight in his face. "Anything," and then she smiled at McFarlane too. He turned and went hastily out of the door.

One floor below they went through the double doors where Probate Court used to be. The room was pretty much the same, except for the bannister, which was gone, and the witness stand. However, the judge's bench had been kept in place, and that's where Councilman Sump was sitting. He was in the middle of a sentence, finishing it with the plaintive drone he affected, while he watched Port and McFarlane walk into the room. They walked past the seats for the public—Sump had always thought it was bad politics to have sessions in private—and McFarlane went to the witness table while Port sat down at the side, in one of the press seats. The press wasn't represented that day.

". . . and as soon as the city solicitor can spare us his time we need no longer hold up the committee's procedings," said Sump. Meaning no offense, the plaintive note had taken strong hold now, but the drone had remained the same.

"I'm ready, Councilman." McFarlane looked up at the bench. But Sump wasn't looking at his witness. He was eying Port, who nodded back with an angelic smile. Sump didn't acknowledge it.

"If our city solicitor can now spare us . . ."

"I'm ready. I said I was ready."

Sump looked pained, with just the right hint that he would bear up under it all. "The committee apologizes, not having heard the witness the first time. Please speak up, Mr. McFarlane. Speak up so the public can hear you, because it is the public, Mr. McFarlane, the public whose interests are vitally involved. The function of this committee," and Councilman Sump sat up straight, there being no other members of the committee present, "as servants of our good citizens, is to act as the detergent quality, as the acid bath which removes the filth of disuse from truth. What we want, Mr. McFarlane, is truth scrubbed clean!"

Port looked at the audience and saw they were having a fairly good time. There were some housewives with shopping bags, and one of the women was massaging her shoeless foot. One or two bums sat in the back, a man in a frayed overcoat taking constant notes, high-school kids, and a farmer from out of town who thought this was still the Probate Court.

"This committee has submitted the question to you, Mr. Counsellor: whether relocation of tenement dwellers has taken into account the will of the public. I am referring to our list of particulars—a copy is here in my hand—which your office has had under advisement for the past two months. Have you, Mr. McFarlane, seen the list of particulars?"

"I have."

"Then why, why has this committee received no answer?"

McFarlane played it straight. He opened a folder and referred to notes. "On May twenty-seventh, last year, my office passed ruling on a resolution dealing with eviction and reimbursement of parties residing in the Highland area where, at the time, our new throughway was being built. Our ruling was posited on the spirit of eminent domain. When your list of particulars was submitted we referred you to that earlier ruling—our reply was filed on a Wednesday, which was two days after your submission—since in our opinion . . ."

"In your *opinion?*"

"That's what you asked for, wasn't it?"

Sump lowered his eyes, sad now, and spoke like a father confessor. "Mac, you and I know, don't we, that opinion can never replace hard, crystal-clear facts?"

"I fail to see the relevance—"

"You fail to see?" Sump was roaring a full, righteous roar. "You fail, Counsellor—you fail in your office of trust, is my answer! Now then, let's get at the facts as we find them. On that Monday, when the committee submitted to you the list of particulars—this list of particulars—" Sump held his copy high—"on that Monday—just where were you?"

"I beg your pardon?"

"Not *my* pardon, Mr. McFarlane!" After allowing it to reverberate Sump lowered his voice, off-handed now. "You are an elected official of the city government?"

"No, sir. My office is filled by appointment."

"Oh. Appointment. And when you were appointed, I'm merely guessing now, but when you were appointed, were you not appraised of the various duties contingent . . ."

"I have been city solicitor for the past twelve years, Mr. Councilman. During the entire time of my tenure . . ."

"You're interrupting."

"Mr. Sump!"

"I hear you talking, Mac, but you haven't said a thing."

There was a silence, noticed by all, and then Sump got down to the part that made him famous.

"Without the flim-flam, now, McFarlane, don't you think it funny that a man in your position should display a guilty conscience as easily as you just did?"

"I didn't display anything of the sort!"

"You weren't shouting? You sit there in the eyes of the public gathered behind you, and have the gall to say, in the face of the facts . . ."

"I mean to say . . ."

"You mean! Just what do you mean?"

"Your assumption of guilt is ridiculous," McFarlane said very quietly.

"Facts are ridiculous?" Sump swelled, and then he started declaiming. Port had had enough and got up. He walked down the length of the room, to the door in back, and when he was halfway there he turned and looked at Sump on the judge's bench. Sump saw him but didn't interrupt the crescendo he was building to when Port jerked his head. Sump went on for a moment, and then got up. "This session will not be terminated until the facts have been shown! I'll be back in a minute." He walked out the door which once had led to the judge's chambers.

Port met him in the hall. Sump was shorter than Port, and had a way of looking up as if he expected to be slapped. "What do you want?" he said.

"I want the crystal-clear truth, Mr. Chairman."

"Why don't you shut up?" said Sump.

Port said, "I want you to come up to the third floor with me. I got something for you. For the committee."

They walked up the stairs and down the hall.

"Make it snappy," said Sump. "I have a hearing downstairs."

"I know," said Port.

They went into the office where Miss Trent was sitting. She looked up with a smile and Sump straightened his tie.

"Why, Mr. Sump," she said. "What are you doing in the enemy's camp?"

Sump straightened his tie.

Port picked the box with the papers off the desk and said, "Thanks for keeping it for me."

She said, "Anything," and watched Port walk out of the office.

When Sump had closed the door Port gave him the carton. He took a questionnaire off the top and said, "I hold here in my hand . . ."

"Why don't you shut up?" said Sump again.

"It's a questionnaire. They all are. Answered and signed by the voters in Ward Nine. Since your committee will introduce debate on the slum clearance thing, you'll want to know all about this. The voice of the public, you know. Is that crystal-clear?"

Sump put the box on the floor, because it was getting heavy.

"There are three questions," said Port. "One: Would you allow the city to increase your expenses? Two: Would you move to better housing if it cost you one third more than you are paying now? Three: Would you be willing to pay up to twice as much more for your utilities? The answers are *no* to all questions, in ninety-nine per cent of the cases."

"What is this?" said Sump.

"Slum clearance cannot take place unless the city pays fifty per cent of the cost for installing utilities, and the city won't do it."

"I haven't heard anything about . . ."

"You will. That leaves the move up to the slum dwellers themselves. If they want to foot the bill, fine. But they won't. Here's their answer."

Sump stared at Port, then picked up the whisky carton. "You've got it sewed up, haven't you?"

"That's the truth, scrubbed clean," said Port and walked to the stairs.

Chapter Seven

WHEN Port came out of Municipal Building he saw the man standing at the bottom of the stairs with one elbow on the front foot of the marble lion. The man had a lined face and simple eyes. He was waiting for Port.

"Landis," said Port. "I thought you went back to legitimate law."

"May I see you, Daniel?"

They went across the street to the restaurant where judges and bondsmen hung out.

"You drink coffee, don't you?" said Landis. They took a booth and ordered coffee for Port and a small beer for Landis.

"How's the Reform movement?" said Port.

"I'm sure you know better than I do," said Landis.

"I just asked, seeing you started it."

"Yes. Not that it shows any more."

"That's Bellamy for you. One great fixer, Bellamy. Why'd you ever take him in, Landis?"

"Inexperience. However, it won't happen again."

Port looked over the rim of his cup. "You still in the game?"

Landis had a trim gray mustache, and he rubbed it with his finger. "First of all, Port, this is not a game. It is not, I think, even a game for you. And second, I wouldn't have started the movement if I didn't think it had the strength to achieve eventually what its name suggests."

"Have it your way," said Port.

"I will."

Landis sipped cold beer and Port drank some cold coffee. Then he said, "I'm sure you wanted something, Landis."

"I saw you inside," said Landis, "at the Sump performance."

"Funny, wasn't it?"

44

"Hardly. I was surprised to see you, Port, because I had heard you were leaving."

"I didn't."

"Why? Pressure, or misguided loyalty?"

"What's the difference?"

"Yes. Anyway, I wondered if you would tell me this, Port. Are you back for good, or is this just temporary?"

"Why do you ask, Landis?"

"Your presence in town makes a difference. I told you quite frankly that I wasn't through, and I tell you just as frankly that my plans for the Reform party would differ, depending on whether or not you are here."

"You'll never make a politician, Landis."

"Wouldn't you figure out what I told you yourself?"

"On second thought, you might make a good one."

"Would you answer my question?"

"Why should I?"

"I thought you might, as long as it doesn't do damage to you or to your loyalties."

"You flatter me, Landis."

"No. I appreciate you."

"Then please appreciate that I won't give you an answer."

Landis nodded his head, but he wasn't through. "Would you tell me this much, Port. Do you intend staying indefinitely?"

Port lit a cigarette and blew the smoke into the aisle. "You know something, Landis, you're taking a lot of liberties. What makes you think I'd give you information that you could use?"

"Because I know as well as you do that basically you don't give a damn what goes on in this town." Landis put out a hand and said, "May I have one of your cigarettes?" They didn't talk while Landis lit up. Then he said, "Or maybe you do. Maybe that's why you were leaving."

Port didn't answer.

"Well?" and Landis put his head to one side.

Port sat back, felt around in an inside pocket. He put some envelopes on the table, a travel folder, and two membership cards. He put everything back in his pocket except for one of the envelopes. He opened it and took out his airplane ticket.

"I bought this. You see? One way out. Take it, Landis," and when Landis held it in his hand Port got up.

Landis said, "All right," and tapped the ticket against one nail. He watched Port pull down his jacket and turn to go.

"If I ask you for it—then you know," said Port and walked away.

"I'll hold on to it," said Landis, but Port was too far away to hear.

Ramon fixed his tie in front of the mirror and looked at it to see if it was quiet enough. It wouldn't do to wear the wrong color, or too much of it, or even to indicate that he had given it thought. He looked sideways at Shelly. She was wearing an apron over her dress, and she was humming.

"How about it," he said. "You almost done with that sink?"

She gave him a smile and stopped the humming. "You worry too much, Nino. I'll be done long before your Mr. Port comes in. You look very nice," she added.

He didn't appreciate the remark and waited till she had turned back to the sink. Then he spat in his palm and smoothed it along one side of his hair.

"And you gotta change yet," he said after a moment.

Shelly wiped her hands dry and went to the stove.

"I'll be out before he gets here," she said, but that wasn't what Ramon had meant.

"You stay here." There was more force behind his voice than he had expected, but Shelly didn't seem to notice. She picked up the percolator with the hot coffee and poured some of it into a little pot.

"You'll be all right," she said. "You're too eager, Nino." She had her back turned to him, so she didn't see his angry frown.

After a while he said, "I wish you'd stay, Shelly. You know, just to be polite."

"But it's business," she said.

"You can always leave later."

She went to the door of her room and said, "What do you want me to wear?"

He shrugged and looked at the oilcloth on the kitchen table. "You know better than I. Just look right, you know?"

She wasn't sure that she knew what he meant, but she knew how anxious he was. She closed the door to her room and started to change into something else. Nino had always been anxious, but then it hadn't mattered. Nino had never done anything. Now it was different. He was doing something, or perhaps someone else was doing something to Nino. She didn't know which.

She heard the knock at the door outside, and when her dress had stopped rustling around her ears she heard chairs scraping at the kitchen table, and Nino laughing. It didn't sound as if there had been a joke, but Nino laughed, said something, laughed again. The other one hadn't said a thing. Shelly buttoned up, shook her hair back, and went to the kitchen.

The first thing Port saw was that she wasn't wearing a red carnation. He said hello to her and he said he hoped she didn't mind his taking up her quarters, but what he was really thinking had to do with the flower. I must bring her a flower, he thought. He frowned and looked at Ramon.

"Shelly," said Ramon, "pour us some coffee, will you?"

Shelly went to the stove. "If you'd like to be alone, Mr. Port, I can . . ."

"Just for a while. Do you mind?"

"You can go in the other room," said Ramon.

"I'll tell you," Port took his cup from her and put it down on the table. "We'll finish this and then your brother and I can go someplace else. I didn't mean to . . ."

"Oh, no!" Ramon laughed. "You go out, Shelly, and come back in half an hour. Okay? Okay, Dan?"

Port said, "Fine," and picked up his cup.

Shelly took a handbag off a hook in the wall and went toward the door. When she passed her brother's chair she touched his shoulder, and when he looked up she smiled at him and said, "I'll see you later." She nodded at Port and opened the door.

"Thanks for the coffee," said Port. He smiled at her and she stood in the door for a moment, smiling back at him. "That was nice of you," he said. She nodded and went out.

Ramon had the feeling they had made quite a lot of that coffee bit. He wished that she could have stayed. Maybe they knew each other better than he thought? Maybe, that thing about having met on the street— He put his cup down.

"What happened with the job?" Port asked.

"I went to the agency, as you said to, and before they sent me out there I memorized those references that were on the card they had ready . . ."

"The job, Ramon."

"I got it."

Port sat back and took a breath and said, "Good."

"It's from eight to five, and they want me to room out there. A room they got in the basement. Their name is Bellamy."

"I know that."

"Oh." Then Ramon waited.

"You know who Bellamy is?"

"I didn't know it was *the* Bellamy. The way you said it . . ."

"It's him."

Ramon felt suspended, even a little shaky, and he didn't know whether it was from eagerness or from fear. But he knew for sure that he was now very important.

Port was drawing a square on the paper and pointed at it.

"Here's your room. Your bed stands over here, and there is a washstand, so, and a table."

"How—how did you know?"

"The electrician that worked at the house yesterday told me." Port took a sip from his cup, then looked up. "You starting tomorrow?"

"Yes. They want me to start tomorrow."

Port drew again.

"Next time you go there lie down on your bed, reach down where the floor board is, here, and pull it away from the wall. It'll pull away easy. Reach in by the corner and there is an earphone."

"Earphone?"

"Yeah. The cord's long enough so you can lie on the pillow and listen with the earphone next to your ear."

"I'll be damned."

"Yeah. Now I don't care about any calls but the ones Bellamy makes, or gets. He's got a daughter, but she isn't likely to use the phone we rigged. She has her own. Now, Bellamy doesn't get in till around nine. I want you to get your sleep between five, when you get off, and nine when he gets in. Tapping is a tiresome job. Watch it you don't fall asleep while you lie there listening. Sometimes nothing happens at all."

Ramon nodded. His mouth was open.

"Bellamy does business on the phone till late at night. He always has. Most of the stuff I don't care about. He's got deals in construction, he talks to New York about fighter contracts, boxing and wrestling; forget it. What I want is local. Whom does he talk to about the Reform party, what does he say, what about Stoker, plans, meetings, what is said about the new tie-up with slum clearance . . ."

"It's—you tied it up again?"

"He'll be talking about that. Some, anyway. But whatever it is, in this connection, listen hard. Write it down if you can't remember, but don't write it down if you can help it. Get names, names of outfits, anything that can tie down the place he is calling, like a club or an office. You got this clear, Ramon?"

Ramon nodded seriously and repeated what Port had said. Port balled up the paper and threw it into a trash carton under the sink. Then he told Ramon how to get in touch with him. Unless it sounded hot he should not use the phone booth that stood at the intersection a short walk from the house, never to use any phone inside the house, but he should talk to the mailman that came to Bellamy's at around nine in the morning. "He's an old one. If he says to you tomorrow, 'Been digging up any worms?' that's him."

"Been digging up any worms," said Ramon. He nodded to himself and looked nervous.

"When's your day off?"

"Uh—Thursday. But not this Thursday."

"He's always been a cheapskate," said Port. He smiled at Ramon. "How much you making?"

"Thirty-five, with room and board."

"That's why he keeps changing the help. He won't pay a real professional."

"His daughter hired me."

"How much does a real gardener make?"

"I don't know. I don't know nothing from gardening. It worries me, you know? You ever think of that?

"You won't be there long enough."

"Oh."

"Do a good job, Ramon, and you're in."

Ramon lit up, but the real relief didn't show in his face until a few moments later, when a key turned in the door and Shelly came in. She said, "If I'm too early . . ."

"No, this is fine," said Port, and noticed that Ramon relaxed. "I'm just going. I apologize," he started when Ramon got up and said he wouldn't have it, that Port should stay. His sister would want him to stay and she should slice up some of the cake she had made.

"I don't know if Mr. Port . . ."

"I like cake," said Port.

He stayed in his chair and watched Shelly slice cake. He saw her from the back and the curve of her back made him think of the girl in McFarlane's office, but he liked this girl better. Or her looks, anyway, since he didn't know Shelly at all.

Ramon was running around, looking in drawers and on shelves and then he said, "I'll be right back. I can't find the cigarettes."

"Use mine," said Port, but Ramon was at the door, explaining that he only smoked one kind and Port's wasn't it. He closed the door and was gone.

They both looked at the door and then Shelly came to the table.

"You still want the cake?"

Port looked up at her and saw what she meant.

"I don't think he'll be back so soon," he said.

Shelly sat down at the table and pushed the cake out of the way. The movement showed the inside of her arm and she moved so slowly that Port thought he was looking at it a very long time. He didn't care if she noticed. She folded her arms on the table and he didn't notice how she looked at him. When she talked he looked up quickly.

"He is trying very hard."

"Ramon? Yes, he is."

"He won't be back for a while, so there's time for me to ask you something."

Port went to the stove and poured himself another cup of coffee.

"What do you want from my brother?"

"It's mutual," said Port. "I need talent, and he wants to give it."

"He has no talent. All he has is big dreams of how to be an operator."

"I won't strain his talents."

"How about his self-respect?"

Suddenly Port didn't like her. He thought her eyes were too large, her fingers too long, and her face had the toneless color of a dark complexion without enough sun.

"He can take it or leave it. So can you."

She poked at the cake with the long knife she was holding, but she kept looking at him.

"You've harmed him already," she said. "He's never done this before."

"What's that?"

"Pimp his sister."

Port put out his cigarette.

"I didn't take him up on it," he said.

Her eyes got narrow and she put down the knife. But her voice was as even as ever.

"You stayed, didn't you?"

Port sat still, letting the tension turn to a physical sting on his skin.

"I would have stayed anyway," he said.

"That's how you planned it?"

"No," he felt irritable with her suspicion. "I just decided. I took one look at that cake of yours . . ."

She jumped up so fast he thought she had in mind leaping at him. He watched how her breasts moved with her breathing and then the color that darkened her face.

"Get out," she said.

He pushed back his chair and got up. Her emotion surprised him.

"And now what, you scream?"

She didn't answer. She picked up the knife and held the point into the oilcloth. Port went to the door, opened it, and turned back to the girl.

"I'll see you," he said.

She punched the knife into the oilcloth again, but didn't move otherwise. Only her face was full of life. "You know," she said, "I don't know how to throw this. If I knew how to throw a knife, I would."

"I'm glad you can't," he said and walked away without closing the door. Shelly could hear him whistling.

Chapter Eight

WHEN Port got to the Lee building the nightman opened the door for him. "Mr. Stoker ain't in," he said, "if that's who you want."

"Where did he go?" Port said.

"He never came in today. Fries was here, but he's gone by now."

Port went back to his car. He leaned against the rear fender and jiggled the antenna that stuck out at an angle. He hoped Stoker hadn't left town for some reason, but he didn't think Stoker would, not at this time. He got into his car.

When he got to the apartment, Mrs. Stoker opened the door. She gave him a hostile look and told him which door to take.

Port knocked at the door and waited till it was opened by Fries, who stepped aside to let Port come in. Stoker was in bed.

There was a knee desk in front of him, a phone by his elbow, and his color was fresh, which—in a case like Stoker's—didn't mean health.

"If it's good, tell him," said Fries. "If it isn't, don't hang around here till you've fixed it."

Port said hello and sat down near the bed. "You've got a good man here," he said to Stoker. "It proves we all got a good side, no matter how bad the first impression is." Then he smiled at Fries.

"One day, horse around like that," said Fries, "and you're gonna be . . ."

"Fries, there's no such thing as a spontaneous ulcer, but you're working on it," Port said.

"All right," said Stoker, "all right, all right—"

"What if a real catastrophe should happen to you," Port went on, "then what could you do? Burst into flame?"

Fries had a lot of control. It killed his appetite, made

him gassy, gave him shooting pains in the back—but none of this showed, which was the point. He said, "You and I must have a talk some day."

"Another one?"

"Another kind."

"If you're both through performing," said Stoker, "before I die from a couple of things that've got nothing to do with my heart—"

"Okay," said Port. "All right if I smoke?"

"Makes no difference," said Stoker.

Port lit up. "I think we've got the ward for a while longer, maybe."

Nobody expected it, not even Fries. He got out of his chair and started to bellow.

"Maybe!" A vein jumped out on his forehead, thick blue, and he was hoarse. "A while longer, maybe! You got an idea that's enough? You got an idea you do us a favor sticking around while you feel like it and swing a little deal on the side so maybe it works and maybe it don't? Now get this straight, Port, and you listen too, Max! There's been a lot of horsing around here doing some greasing now and then, or a pep talk now and then, when it looked like business might get out of hand. That's not good enough now! We got the machine in this town, and we can make it hum. But you gotta first throw the right lever, and believe me, Port, that takes muscle!"

Fries stopped with a hard breath in his throat, and then he sat down. He looked away for a moment, rubbing his mouth, as if he were afraid it might start screaming again. Stoker sat still in his bed and Port looked at him.

"What was that?" he said, and the surprise in his face was real.

Fries was back to normal when he said to Port, "If you're going to start making jokes again . . ."

"He won't." Stoker might have felt sick, but he didn't sound it. Fries closed his mouth and Port listened. "Three of his men got into a brawl."

"Got jumped," said Fries.

"Three of his men got jumped. That's why he's talking that way."

"If Bellamy thinks . . ."

"I think they're imports," said Port. "The three I was talking to were suntanned, and who do you know in this town, this time of year, who've got suntans."

"Very clever," said Fries. "I'm really impressed. Most of all by the way you figured that out. They had suntans!" To Fries it didn't sound funny. The tic came back into one of his eyes and he said, "That Reform Party started to roll when Bellamy took it over. Next thing you know he bulldozed right over everything our brain-truster here ever set up. And next thing you know, he imports hoods. The difference between . . ."

"I'll tell you the difference," said Stoker. "Some places it's muscle, other places that doesn't work. That's the difference, but Bellamy doesn't know it. He starts heaving muscle in this game and maybe starts thinking that's all he needs . . ."

"What makes you think he's got no brains?"

"The first real move he made," said Port. "That's what makes me think so."

"Listen." Fries showed how little he liked being contradicted. "If you mean that newspaper release, it pretty near wrecked us. For all you've said around here, it's still got us running."

"If you'll listen a minute, Fries." Port pulled out his cigarettes. "His first big move is a dumb move. He throws it around to the public that we bribed the Planning Board. So we did. So what. To make hay on that, there's got to be two things. One, we have to give him an argument so the public can get involved; two, he's got to be ready with something to follow it up, some concrete thing that shows him to be better than us. He didn't have it. All he had was a lot of political hogwash hung on to his revelations. So there's Bellamy yelling robbers, but he isn't making a move to chase 'em himself." Port looked at Fries. "That makes him dumb. Remember that, Fries."

Stoker rolled over in bed and closed his eyes as if he were tired. "I want to hear what you did about it."

Port told him. He explained what he did with McFarlane and with Councilman Sump. There wasn't a chance for the city to tear down the slums and ruin Boss Stoker's Ward Nine. It sounded complete and final.

"You satisfied?" said Stoker from the bed.

"You'll have to watch it to see what they do next."

"Who do you mean by 'you'?" said Stoker.

Port didn't answer, so Stoker went on.

"Let's say I ask Fries to watch it. What should he be watching for?"

"He's an old hand," said Port.

"Let's say Fries keeps watching Bellamy's hoods, so his monkeys don't get clobbered when they drink beer some place."

"That would be bad," said Port.

"What should I be watching?" asked Fries.

Port ignored the tone and answered him.

"Stalling the slum clearance can work for years, but it's never better than stalling. After a while there won't be any slums."

"You sound like Landis," said Fries.

"He's got brains."

"Let's stick to the point," said Stoker. "What happens now?"

"We stalled them on a legal gimmick. An interpretation. So the next move from Reform should be a re-interpretation."

"State Capitol?" Stoker asked.

"I don't know. Maybe they can do it locally."

"I can handle that. But I'm not good enough to handle the Capitol."

"They haven't gotten that far yet. Maybe they never will."

"But what if they do? We gotta have the next step all laid out. We can't . . ."

"Leave me out of it, Max." Port got up.

Stoker turned on his back.

"Danny."

"What do you want from me?" The other two men looked up. "You want a thirty-year contract or something? Or an oath? I told you before what you're going to get from me. I'm through explaining. I don't run out, and I don't leave you a mess. There won't be any loose ends when I'm through, and I'm going to be through when they vote down the clearance project. And meantime don't keep pushing at me or dreaming up extra work to take home nights." H₂ went to the door and said, "I'm going to bed."

Boss Stoker stopped him.

"There's a new arrangement," he said, "because of Bellamy and his new methods."

Port waited, keeping his hand on the door knob.

"Beginning tomorrow you don't go out except with protection. You got a gun?" Stoker continued.

"I always sleep with a gun under my pillow."

Stoker ignored it.

"Fries will send over a man in the morning. He goes with you."

Port said, "Go to hell," and slammed the door shut.

Chapter Nine

WHEN Port got out of the shower he heard the telephone in the next room. It was barely past eight in the morning. He stopped toweling himself and picked up the phone. The voice started right in, "Hello, hello? That you, Dan?"

"Yeah."

"Dan, this is Ramon."

"Where you calling from, damn it?"

"The booth down at the corner from Bellamy's place—"

"All right, what is it?"

"This morning, maybe five, ten minutes ago, I just happened to pick up the receiver—I don't go to work till nine, you know—and there's Bellamy talking."

"About what?"

"I didn't listen long enough, Dan, I thought you ought to know who the other guy was."

"All right, who?"

"McFarlane! . . . Did you hear me?"

"You said McFarlane."

There was a pause from Ramon, and then he said, "Well, that's it. Isn't he supposed to be in with us? What's he doing having talks with Bellamy?"

Port rubbed his hair with the towel. Then he said, "McFarlane plays both sides of the fence. I thought you knew."

"He does? And you do business with him?"

"Why not? He never gets told anything the other side isn't supposed to know, and meanwhile he delivers."

Ramon was glad that Port couldn't see him.

"Christ, I thought—I'm sorry I called for nothing."

"Don't worry about it."

"Really, Dan, if I had known . . ."

"As long as you didn't know, you did right."

"If you say so."

"Now get back there and dig in the garden."

Ramon said good-by and hung up, but the thing stayed with him for quite a while longer.

Port forgot about it and got dressed. When he got downstairs and walked out on the street a man pushed away from the wall of the building and said, "Bang." Then he grinned.

For a minute Port thought he'd murder the guy, but then he took a deep breath and rubbed his hands so they would stop shaking.

Simon laughed. "You see, Danny, Max was right. You do need protection."

Port came up with a long string of profanity, repeating himself several times and inventing some new things. Simon waited. When Port was through Simon said, "That was beautiful. Are you through?"

"You're through. Now beat it!"

But Stoker had picked the right man, because Simon could not be impressed. He could be told what to do; after that it was hard to get to him, and when it was contradictory there was no use talking to him at all. "I could beat the stuffing out of you and leave you on the street," said Port.

"No, you couldn't."

Port knew this was true.

"Look, Simon, you're too slow. I can't use you. What if something comes up all of a sudden, I get jumped, for instance . . ."

"I'm good from close in."

This was true too. Simon had the nervous system of a slow worm. It made him sluggish, but it also made him immune to pain. With Simon the other man always got off the first punch. After that—when the other man slowed down in surprise—is when Simon paid off. He could hit, and he could last, like granite.

"All right, come on," said Port. "But keep out of my way."

"What you say, Danny?" Port didn't bother to answer and kept still all the way to the club, where he went into a room with a desk and a typewriter. A club member was sleeping in the swivel chair and Port told Simon to throw him out. Simon did this. Then Port told Simon to leave the room and to let nobody in. Port wasn't bothered for the next five hours. He put typing paper and carbon into the machine and typed almost continuously. Sometimes he stopped, closed his eyes while he got things straight, and then he would write again. Part of the time Simon could hear Port whistling.

When Port finished he addressed an envelope and called Simon. "Run down to the office in front and get Phil up here. He should bring his notary public thing. And if you see Lantek tell him to come up, too. If you don't see him, bring anyone."

Simon came back with Lantek and Phil, who had brought his notary public stamp.

"All you guys stand over there by the wall. Can you see me writing?" Port took a desk pen and made passes at the sheets in front of him, as if he were writing.

"You're making passes at the paper there," said Simon. Lantek nodded and so did Phil. They couldn't read the typing, but they could see where Port started to sign each page in the margin. The last page he signed on the bottom. He turned the pile over, blank side up, and had Phil sign his notary spiel and apply his stamp. Under that he got the two others to witness the notarizing. He did this with each sheet. When it was done he sent them all out again. Port sealed the original into the envelope and fastened the carbon together with a paper clip. He put those two things, and the carbon paper, into his pocket. When Port went downstairs, Simon followed him.

"What did you write, Danny?"

"Last will and testament, seeing you're here to protect me."

Simon laughed at that. He was still laughing when Port stopped at the curb outside.

"Take my car," said Port, "and run down to Tucker Street. I'll wait for you here while you pick . . ."

"That means you're staying here alone!"

There was a short pause by both of them, but after a moment Port started to walk to his car. Simon followed. When they turned into Tucker Street Simon couldn't wait any longer. "I know you don't want to talk to me, Danny, but I'm getting hungry. For me it's way past lunchtime right now. I'm wondering . . ."

"I noticed you got kind of lively," said Port. "We'll eat right now."

Simon was pleased until he saw where Port stopped and where he went in, because a flower shop wasn't what Simon expected. Port came back with a short-stemmed red carnation and Simon didn't say a word. They drove back to Ward Nine, parked near the club, and Port led the way to the beanery with the grocery counter in front. The special was corned beef hash patties with a fried egg, and a tomato salad. They ordered that and sat at a table. Simon sat facing the door, since he took his job seriously, and Port sat facing the back. Shelly wasn't there. The fat grocer served them. Port ate with one hand, holding the flower in the other.

"Danny, I don't mean to be personal," said Simon, "but the flower—"

"You like it?"

"Just don't hold it the way you do, Danny. I'm eating corned beef and smelling carnation."

Port moved the flower and they finished eating. Shelly still hadn't showed up.

The door opened and a girl came in. Port couldn't see her because he was facing the other way, but he guessed that it was a girl from Simon's expression. They both watched her pass to the counter where she sat on a stool. They had a good view. Port missed seeing Shelly come in from the back, and he missed what she did. Shelly stopped in the back door when she saw Port and took off the red carnation she had on her lapel. She put it behind the counter.

Then the girl on the stool turned around and got up. She came to the table and said, "You're Danny Port, ain't you?"

"Sit down, sit down," said Simon and pulled out a chair for her. She sat without looking at Simon, and then Port remembered. She had worn only a blouse and shoes, and eight men had been with her.

"You don't remember? I was up in the club, with eight of 'em."

"Sure, I remember. How's it been—"

"Kate."

"How's it been, Kate?"

"What you mean, eight of 'em?" Simon wanted to know.

"I'm a hooker," said Kate and turned back to Port.

He twirled the stem of the flower between two fingers, and tried to catch Shelly's eye. When she looked at him he smiled, but she didn't give it back. "Three coffees," he called, and then looked back at Kate.

"You working?" he asked her.

Shelly came over with three cups of coffee and put them down without saying a word. Port kept twirling the red carnation, kept trying to look at her, but Shelly looked elsewhere. When she was gone and Port picked up his cup it seemed to him he'd never had coffee that hot before.

"I'm not working," said Kate. She had a careless face and a careless body, and when she leaned back in her chair Simon spilled coffee down his chin.

"I come to thank you," said Kate, "for the way you treated me."

"Sure, Kate."

"They coulda throwed me out without paying, except you told them to."

"You're welcome, honey."

She looked at Port for a moment, as if she were waiting for more. Then she said, "I come to thank you."

Port smiled at her and said, "Good," because he thought she had said thank you often enough.

Simon leaned over the table and sounded as if he had a raw throat. "She means in trade, for God's sakes. She wants to pay you back in trade."

"Kate, you don't owe me a thing."

"I think so."

"Dan," said Simon, "*she* thinks so. What in hell is the matter with you?"

Kate said, "Ain't that Shelly's flower? Shelly always . . ."

"Not yet," said Port, and stopped twirling the carnation between his fingers. "I haven't given it to her yet."

"Is she watching?" said Kate.

"No."

"So why don't you go out and wait at the car. Where's your car?"

"Honey, I said no."

Kate looked from one to the other, not knowing what to do next. "So how am I gonna return the favor?"

Port didn't know what to say, and Simon couldn't talk. He was grinning, biting his lip, and his eyes looked wet.

"He a friend of yours?" and Kate nodded at Simon.

"Quite a while now."

"Maybe you owe him a favor."

Simon, at special times, could be very fast. He said,

"Does he! He owes me favors from way back. Danny, don't you remember from way back the favors you . . ."

"Okay then," said Kate. She got up and waited for Simon, who almost knocked over the table.

Port said, "Jeesis," and watched them go out of the door.

After a while he called to Shelly that he wanted another coffee and when she came the first thing he saw was that she was wearing a red carnation. She put his fresh cup down and picked up the three old ones.

"I brought you this," said Port and held up the flower. "I thought . . ."

"I got one."

"Yours is wilted, Shelly."

"I don't think so. I think the one I have is fine."

"Then wear two. One here, and one there."

She didn't answer, and took the used cups back to the counter. Port got up and went to sit on a stool. Shelly turned to look down at him.

"Would you like something else?" She could look mean as hell.

"Sure."

"No," she said. "Like the first time, on the street."

Port grinned and smelled the flower.

Shelly turned away to clean up the grill, which was already clean. It made her feel silly after a while, and there was a place on her back that started to itch.

"Look," she said, "just because you got my brother to take jumps and make cartwheels for you, don't think . . ."

"I'm not thinking of your brother. I'm sitting here looking at you, and it's got nothing to do with your brother."

She glared at him, because he was looking at her and there wasn't a thing she could do. She drew herself a coke and started to sip it. She leaned against the ice cream tank behind her, crossed her legs, and folded her arms.

"When you get real impatient," she said, "why don't you go out and find Kate. She'll take anything."

"Don't slam Kate. At least she knows what she's got."

Shelly felt like hiding. She recrossed her legs and her thoughts made her furious.

"You know," said Port, "right now I'm just sitting here, waiting for Simon to get back. I thought at first you and me could have a visit while I was waiting. But right now I'm just waiting for them to get back."

She was working her teeth into her lower lip, which

made her look like an animal. Port massaged the palms of his hands. "When I first came in, I just wanted to give you this flower."

"All right, give it to me," and she stepped up to the counter. She took her flower off and dropped it into the sink, but didn't reach for the new one. She had her arms by her side, leaned forward a little, and nodded down at herself. "Go ahead. You put it on."

Port got up, smiled at her, and said he was glad to do that.

"No, not the lapel. Where the pocket is."

She said it with her eyes narrowed, and Port did the job with the flower carefully. Then he sat down.

"You should appreciate this," he said. "I've never done that before."

"I could tell." She leaned back against the ice cream tank and took off the flower. She moved it up to pin it where it belonged. "But you learn fast. Just don't forget what you learn."

Port got up and paid his check.

"The next lesson, I give," and he walked out.

Chapter Ten

PORT stood on the street for a while and looked across to the club. His car wasn't there any more so he walked down the block a short way to look into the empty lot. His car and a few others were there. He smoked a cigarette, and walked around for fifteen minutes. Simon didn't show. Port went into the lot. He figured by this time his body-guard needed some saving.

Simon was in the back. He was on his stomach, sprawled out limp, and the lump on the back of his head showed plainly. Kate wasn't there.

Port got Simon into a sitting position, but Simon was still out. Port started to snap his finger under the limp man's nose, which woke Simon after a while.

"You look exhausted, Simon. Let me tell you."

Simon groaned and took the cigarette Port handed to him.

"As a matter of fact, Simon, I'm going to ask Fries to assign a man to you, somebody that'll follow you no matter what. Then, maybe . . ."

"Danny, please. Don't yell so loud."

Port slid behind the wheel, then turned back again. "I'm going to start the motor. You think the vibration will be too much for you?"

"Danny, what am I gonna say? What are you gonna tell Fries about this?"

"Nothing. But you tell me something. How did she do it? How did that little bitty girl . . ."

"Oh, Christ—" moaned Simon.

"At least tell me this, Simon."

"I don't know. So help me I can't remember!"

Simon looked down at his knees. "I know I was doing all right there. Just for a while."

"Then what did she do?"

64

"I don't know. I thought that she was doing all right too."

"Anyway," and Port turned to start the car, "at least she doesn't owe me anything any more."

"I don't know, Danny. I think she still does."

The rest of the day Port spent in different places. He dropped in on McFarlane, checked progress with Councilman Sump, spent some time at the club in Ward Nine when a local matter came up there, and he mailed the envelope with the sheets he had typed in the morning. He sent it, registered, to an address in New York, requesting a return receipt. When he got home at night he put the carbon copy into his trunk. He sat smoking for a while in the dark, because that way he could see out the window. He imagined he wouldn't see this view for much longer, because when the council voted down the slum resolution that would be that. Just a few days, maybe. He went to bed and was asleep in a very short time. . . .

He didn't think he had slept very long. He sat up, in the dark, and heard the knock on the door again. When he got out of bed the voice said, "It's me," and it knocked again. Port switched on the lamp by his bed and put on a bathrobe. Then he opened the door.

"You alone?" said Kate.

"That's real delicate of you," said Port. He stepped aside to let her in. "Where's your blackjack?"

"I don't carry no blackjack." She walked in and put her purse down on a chair. She put her hands on her hips and waited for Port to close the door. "What would I need a blackjack for?"

Port looked at her in the light that was coming at her from one side and said, "Yeah. What for is right." Then he sat down on the bed and fixed himself a cigarette.

"Did Simon tell you?" she asked. There was an easy chair near the bed where she sat down.

"No, but he showed me. He showed me the lump on the back of his head and to this moment I can't figure out just how you did it." Port saw she was pushing one shoe off her foot with the other. "You going to show me how it's done?"

"I didn't do it," she said.

Port didn't see her push off the other shoe because he was surprised and looked at her face.

"I thought you were an honest whore, Kate. Dames that play badger games like this I don't like."

"I didn't know the guys did it to him."

Port frowned, and then he saw Kate unbutton her jacket. He said, "Hey—" but then he watched when she slipped it off. She paused after that and frowned back at him.

"Katie, look. I know it's hard as hell for a woman to just take it when I say no to her. So pull yourself together and . . ."

"Whatsa matter with you? Didn't Simon tell you?"

"He got conked. What could he tell me?"

"I still owe you. At least he shoulda knowed what he didn't get."

"No," said Port. He closed his eyes when he said it so Kate was half done by the time he looked back. She had her blouse open and was flapping it back. She did all this with no ado, without doing any more than removing her clothes.

Port got up and took a few steps. Kate looked after him.

"I also come to tell you about them two guys. Something you might have a use for."

"What in hell you going to do? Sit there naked?"

"You don't wear nothing under that robe." She used his tone of voice.

He controlled himself. "What was that, an argument?"

"Who's arguing?" and she unhooked her brassiere in the back.

He stopped arguing and watched what she did. Then he remembered about Simon.

"You were going to tell me something about those two guys."

"Well, they tore open the door and Simon and me were in the back. Simon is kind of slow anyway, so before he got adjusted one of the guys, the short one, gave him a belt."

"On the back of the head?"

"I thought it was coming off."

"Simon wasn't out cold right then?"

"You arguing or listening? Simon tries getting up when the short guy says, 'Just a sample, lamebrain, of what we think of Port and his bodyguard.' Then he slams Simon on the head again. They shut the door and I try getting up from underneath Simon."

She stood up and undid the zipper on the side of her skirt.

"That's it?" said Port.

"Then they came back. 'Might as well,' says one of them and tells me to get out of the car. And they take me to this place." She dropped the skirt and stepped out of it. "You know the apartment house on Birch. Twelve hundred Birch?"

"I know where it is."

"Well, they take me up on the second floor and they got a layout there. What I mean is, not like an apartment, but with phones and bunks and a messy kitchen like there hasn't been a woman in the house—I mean a housewife in the house—for ages."

"So they live there like pigs."

"No. It's like your club. Like some rooms in your club, you know?"

"Who were they, you know?"

"They were none of your ward men. And these had suntans."

Port remembered, and perhaps Kate had told him something. They lived in the ward, and the way Kate had told it, these two weren't the only ones. Not a bad notion for Bellamy to put his hoods down close to the center of things. If he was going to use his new crew, the likeliest place would be Ward Nine. Trouble in Stoker's notorious Ward Nine. Gangsterism and Crime, etc.

"Did you get their names?"

"One was Kirby, the short mean one."

"And George?"

"Maybe. I didn't call them by name."

It made Port smile. Then he said, "Did they pay you?" She shook her head.

"How much are you?"

"Nothing, to you."

"I mean them."

"On my own, I wouldn't have anything to do with them for fifty bucks."

He saw she meant it. He also saw she was kicking her panties off and stood there naked. She stood there as if she didn't know about clothes and no clothes, as if it were all the same. That wasn't the way Port felt when she stepped closer and put her head to one side.

Port tried to speak, but nothing much came of it. Kate noticed and put her hands up to reach for his neck when she suddenly found there was no more distance between them. He didn't have time to turn off the light.

Chapter Eleven

TEN-THIRTY A.M. Simon was still waiting in front of the building. He figured three hours' waiting would be long enough; he would wait till eleven and then go upstairs. He looked down the length of the block to the diner, because he hadn't eaten that day. Then he looked back at the building entrance because that's what he was supposed to do. When he saw Kate come out, it confused him and failed to connect with his mission. She said, "Hi, Simon," and it immediately brought back the past to him. He ran up to her and grabbed her arm. "How did you do it?" he wanted to know. "I can't figure out, and Port can't either."

"Do what?"

"Yesterday. In the car."

"I didn't do anything," she said. "And you didn't either."

Simon held on to her arm and started to think. It made his face sullen. "You know, that makes me mad."

Kate pulled her arm out of his hand. "All right. You had a good time. Now you feel better?"

He kept looking at her, then took her arm again. "There's something here ain't kosher. I had such a good time I got a bump on the back of my head?"

"That wasn't me. I was in front of you."

It connected Simon with the past, and when Kate tried to pull away again Simon held on. His thumb started to rub the soft of her arm.

"No," she said. "I'm tired."

"Hell, it's ten in the morning."

"That's why. Ten in the morning isn't nice," and she pulled her arm out of his hand.

He felt like going after her when Port came out of the door and tapped Simon on the back. "Had your breakfast yet?"

"Where were you?" said Simon. "I been standing here without breakfast or anything."

"I thought you might, and that's why I got up to take you to breakfast." Port took Simon by the arm and they went to the diner. After they ate they had to sit for a while longer because Port's coffee was still too hot.

"You know something?" said Simon. "That hooker, she come outa your building."

"You mean that, Simon?"

"Sure enough. You know, she still owes you that thank you, and I'm going to see to it she pays up."

"Don't bother, Simon. I made an arrangement with her so she won't have to pay."

"What you do that for?"

Port gave a soothing pat to Simon's arm and handed him a cigarette. Then they went for the car and drove toward Ward Nine.

Less than halfway there Simon spotted the girl on the street. "Kate!" he said, and when Port pulled up next to her Simon had the door already open.

"I'm going your way," said Port. "You want a lift?"

She said yes and Simon flipped the back rest forward so she could get in the rear.

"Simon," said Port. "You sit in front."

Simon obeyed but made clear how sore he was by looking out of the window and not talking to anybody.

When Port started the car again Kate caught his eye in the rear-view mirror. She grinned at him and said, "Thank you, Port."

Port stopped the car. He turned around to the back and said, "That's perfectly all right, Kate. It's a common courtesy, and please don't think that you now owe me anything."

She grinned at him again and Port started driving.

When they got to the old streets of Ward Nine, Kate told them where she lived. When they reached her house Simon got out of the car and waited for Kate to pass.

"Now you know where I live," she said to Simon, "come over some time."

She was gone into the house before Simon could answer.

They drove down to the club and Simon went to the room with the easy chairs to toss the volley ball with the two guys that were sitting there. Port went upstairs. At twelve-fifteen he got a call from a gray-haired mailman who for ten minutes repeated for Port all that Ramon had told him that morning. Then he waited while Port didn't say a-thing. After a while Port said, "You sure you got all of it?"

"I'm sure, Dan. Anything in it?"

"I don't know yet."

"In case you're interested, Dan, I got some Special Delivery for that street. You want me to drop in on the boy again?"

Port thought for a moment and then, "It might help. Tell him to come to his house tonight."

"After work?"

"After his real job. I figure there won't be anything after twelve midnight, so I'll expect him around two. At his house."

"I'll tell him," said the mailman and hung up.

There hadn't been much to put your finger on, but Port wrote it all down, because his memory wasn't as good as some. The main thing that struck him was an address, and he would have to ask Ramon how it was mentioned, just what the connection was. The address was 1200 Birch.

This time Port was glad to have Simon along. They walked the few blocks to the apartment building, and in the entrance hall Port checked the names of the tenants. The place was valuable. Three floors with two apartments, each apartment divided in half and half the apartments rented per room. And rent went per person. The place was built of brick, so the upkeep hadn't been very much. The plumbing was galvanized iron or lead, very old, and the upkeep on that was charged to the tenants. With the rents, they didn't have much to complain about.

"I can't find the super," said Port.

They went through the list of twenty-nine people again. This time Port found the name with the gold star behind it. "We'll try her," said Port, and at the end of the ground-floor hall found the door with another gold star pasted on the wood. A sign said: HOURS FROM 11 TO 12 A.M. AND 2 TO 3 P.M.

"She don't leave much room for business," said Simon.

"Her tenants don't have much to complain about." Then Port checked his watch. He was in luck, the time being just after two, and knocked on the door.

A buzzer sounded which made the door spring open a crack. They walked in.

"Pick up your form as you pass that table," said the

voice. Port couldn't tell whether it was a hoarse woman or
a cantankerous man, but it turned out to be a woman, a
large one, half hidden by the chintz wing chair by the
window in back. Port and Simon each picked up a printed
form, reading Tenant Application Form and Waiver of
Liability.

"Step around," said the woman, and they did.

There was a strong odor of roses in the air, the kind that
came in cakes of crystal, sold at the five and dime. Port
was sure that the use of the perfume was no affectation;
it masked plumbing odors.

"Fill out both sides of each page and sign in my presence," said the woman.

"Are you Mrs. Fragonard?" Port asked her.

"I am. And the super."

Simon said, "Gee." Her face looked ageless under rose
powder, and her hair was blue except for the white roots.
But what added the real excitement was the orange robe.
Port saw no lapdog, no parrot, not even a cat. Fish, then,
he thought, but the basin on the window sill at her side
was a terrarium, and the pet inside was a large bullfrog.
He seemed asleep, breathing quickly in and out a few
times and then not at all for several minutes.

"Before we fill this thing out," Port started.

"You better hurry it up. I don't see nobody after three."

"I understand. But . . ."

"I get just overrun with chores and demands if I don't
stick to a regular working day."

"Of course—"

"No time to myself atall, elsewise."

She sat with hands folded in her lap and looked at her
bullfrog.

"You got a room for the two of us?"

"No."

"That's a shame," said Port.

"Fill that out anyways. Come vacancy time you'll be all
set to move in."

"What about this waiver thing, Mrs. Fragonard.
Who . . ."

"That means I don't owe you nothing. I can't be bothered all day long and have my time taken up with chores."

"About paying in cash, Mrs. Fragonard, the fact is, when
I move in I want to pay you by check. The reason . . ."

"Can't do it."

"I don't want to mess with your routine, Mrs. Fragonard, but isn't it dangerous taking that much cash out of here to the bank every week?"

"No trouble to me. They pick it up and . . ."

"Who picks it up?"

She looked away from the bullfrog and gave Port a cold look. It didn't go with the rose powder. "If you think you're casing yourself a caper, young man, let me tell you I work for a big outfit. They don't . . ."

"That's what I wanted to know. Who they are, I mean."

"Why?"

"I won't be here part of the time, to pay rent, but I can send my check to the owners and save you the trouble."

"Now you listen to me . . ."

"Please, Mrs. Fragonard. Of course I'll pay you your deposit. And any surcharges that might accrue."

"In cash."

"Of course."

"The name is Sun Property Management. They have offices . . ."

"I know where," said Port and got up. He put the application form down and then Simon got up and put his down, too. "I'll just look around the premises, Mrs. Fragonard, and come back to sign later."

"I don't see how," she said. "It's near two-thirty, and I'm closing at three. I can't have chores and demands . . ."

"I'll make it in time. Tomorrow."

"Put the forms back on the table," she called after them. They did, and said good-by. She was looking at her bullfrog.

"We moving in here?" said Simon when they were back in the hall.

"She doesn't seem very anxious."

"I don't like her either," said Simon. "A dame's got no business with lizards."

"Bullfrog."

"I mean."

"What did you want her to do, look at you all the time?"

"And why not?"

Port was reading the tenant list and didn't answer. Then he went up the stairs. They stopped in front of a door with the number 22, and Port pulled Simon close. "It's a longish story but I'll tell you all of it, all at once. You remember Kate?"

"What are you talking about, do I remember Kate?"

"In the car yesterday, she didn't do a thing to you. I mean she had nothing to do with that bump on the head."

"I got the bump, don't I?"

"There's two guys in here, Simon, and they hit you. They opened the car door and slammed you on the back of the head."

"Is that so? Why?"

"They saw what you were doing and wanted to stop you."

"They prudes or something?"

"They wanted Katie themselves."

"They did?" Simon started to breathe hard.

"And they did."

"Open up that double damn door," said Simon.

Port knocked on the door.

"Who wants in?" said a voice. Port thought it must be Kirby.

"Mrs. Fragonard," said Port, not worrying that his voice was too low.

"Huh?" And then, "I don't believe it."

Footsteps came to the door and Kirby opened it. He took one look, a smirk came over his face, and he stepped back ceremoniously. "Walk in! While you can walk," he added, and started to laugh.

Simon stepped to one side so Port could go in first, and then he followed without haste. He walked slowly up to Kirby and moved his arm toward Kirby so that it looked like nothing. Kirby collapsed on the floor and Simon shut the door quietly.

"Where's that other bastard?" said Simon.

George was on a couch in back, up on one elbow, and it seemed he had been asleep. He looked at Kirby lying on the floor and blinked. Port had stopped, but Simon was coming across the room. Then George jumped up very quickly. He reached for his jacket hanging on a chair when Port said, "Don't, George." Port had both hands in his pockets and George stopped still.

"What about him!" he said, and watched Simon coming.

"Not yet, Simon. I first gotta ask him something."

Simon stopped, but he was very agitated. He reached for George's coat and tore it straight down the back. Then he tore off the sleeves.

"Don't waste it," said Port.

Simon said, "Ha! You wanna see what I got left? You want me . . ."

"Later, Simon."

George took a deep breath and sat down on the couch again.

"I've come to ask," said Port, "why Bellamy put you here."

"I don't have to tell you nothing."

Simon had a trick of opening and closing his hands so the knuckles cracked. He did this, and George said, "To make a mess here. In the ward."

"When?"

"After the council vote."

"And now I want to ask something else. You know this girl Katie?"

"I don't know no girl Katie."

"Yesterday. The one you took away from my friend Simon."

"Oh," said George and looked at Simon.

"She says you didn't pay her."

George didn't answer because he was watching Simon.

"You owe her," said Port.

"All right. Lemme put my hands in my pocket."

"Fifty bucks," said Port.

"Fifty!"

He meant to say more, but Simon had thrown the chair at him. They gave him a little time and then Simon helped him pull money out of his pocket. There were eighty dollars in bills and Simon took fifty of that and handed it over to Port.

"Now Kirby," said Port.

Simon went over to Kirby, who was out on the floor, and came back with fifty dollars.

"We are leaving now," said Port, "and once your buddy wakes up we want you to do the same. Who else lives here?"

"Five of us. There's five of us Bellamy put here."

"Tell them to leave, too. I'm sending Simon over tomorrow to help you move in case you're still here."

"You gonna be here?" Simon asked.

"No," said George.

"Let's go," said Port and went to the door.

"But what about him?"

"Leave him be, Simon."

"But I ain't through!"

"Kick a chair or something."

Port went out and stood in the hall while Simon made a racket inside. When he came out Port could see the pile of wrecked furniture in the middle of the room.

At ten that night Port went home, because that was the only way he could get rid of Simon. He parked his car and Simon walked as far as the door. Port said, "You going to see Katie tonight?"

Simon nodded.

"Then take her this," and Port handed over the hundred dollars.

He watched Simon take it and fold it with some other bills out of his pocket.

"Where'd you get that pile?" Port asked him.

"After you left. When I was cleaning their room."

"Simon, I never thought of you as a crook."

"It's only fifty, Dan."

"Still—"

"I needed it, Dan. I just told you I'm gonna see Katie."

Port looked at Simon and said, "Oh." He nodded his head and went quickly into the building.

Chapter Twelve

AT TWELVE that night Port reached Ramon's apartment. There was a light in the kitchen which showed under the door, but when he knocked nobody answered. He knocked a few more times and then he tried the door. It opened, but nobody was in.

Port sat down at the kitchen table and waited. There was a coffee pot on the stove, so Port went and poured himself a cup. Then he saw Shelly. He saw her through the half-open door in the next room, where she was lying on a bed, eyes closed. She was on her stomach, breathing regularly, and only her shoes were off. Port put the rest of the coffee back on the stove and lit a flame under the pot. Before he sat down at the table again he went to the room and opened the door enough so he could see her from his chair.

He sat watching her, watching how her bare arm hung over the side of the bed, how the black hair was sprawling all over, and how the curve of her back moved with her breathing.

After a while she frowned, rubbed her face into the pillow, and woke. Port saw there had been a book under her, and when she sat up she rubbed her belly.

"Good evening," said Port.

She looked around, wide-eyed, but if there had been fear it was gone much too soon to tell. She jumped up and came running into the kitchen. She was so mad she couldn't talk. Just when Port was sure she was going to claw him she frowned again and ran to the stove. Port suddenly noticed that the coffee odor was heavy, and when Shelly took the pot off the flame there was nothing left inside the pot but black charcoal. She threw the pot into the sink and came to the table. Her hair was wild, her blouse was half out, the skirt made oblique wrinkles from

77

hips over the belly—and he thought she was magnificent.
Then she put her arms akimbo and yelled.

"Now, get out!"

"I just came."

"I don't want you!"

He shrugged, said, "But I want you."

She glared at him, but the wind was gone out of her. She
bit her lip and tucked in the blouse. It made one of the
buttons pop open in front. She looked down at it and
stamped her foot while Port enjoyed how it bounced her.
Then she ran out of the room.

Port thought he would put on another pot of coffee
while she was gone, but Shelly came back almost immediately. She wore the same things, only this time there was
a big blanket robe over everything.

"I see you're still here," she said.

"I came to see your brother."

"You are lying."

"True. I came courtin'. After that, your brother."

"What?" she said.

"Courting. An old-fashioned term we sometimes use
when we have it in mind."

"I know what you want, but I don't want it."

"I didn't mean now. Besides, your brother will be here
soon. Would you make us another pot of that coffee?"

"When is my brother coming?"

"Around two, I think."

She looked at the clock on a shelf, then back at Port.

"It's not even one yet!"

"Honey, I told you I came courtin'."

She took a deep breath that spread open the robe, and let
the air come out of her throat like a growl. She closed
her eyes for a moment, then looked at Port.

"Now, you listen to me." She stepped up to Port and he
saw that her face was all relaxed, except for the eyes. It
made her look so completely evil that Port had to blink. "I
want one thing from you, to go away and not to come
back. And I know what you want. All right, I'll go to bed
with you and after you're through, don't come back. Right
now," she said, eying him.

He sat down at the table and lit a cigarette. When he
blew smoke it came out a whistle.

"Not now," he said. "I don't like your attitude."

She just stared at him.

"You knew that, didn't you?" he said.

Shelly sat down and looked at the table for a moment. "Yes. But that does not matter."

"You mean for Nino . . ."

"I sleep with whom I like."

"Shelly. You just told me you don't like me."

She leaned toward him, over the table, and Port saw how angry she was.

"You can talk, try to confuse me; it doesn't matter. I can sleep with you and not even know it, and that's how . . ."

"That's what I meant. I don't like that attitude."

He hadn't expected it, not knowing her well, but he saw her sit back, and she was suddenly no longer angry. She looked tired.

"You are very good, trying to confuse me," she said. "Why are you trying?"

"I'm not. I'm just trying to talk to you. Not Ramon's sister. You."

She gave a short laugh, but said nothing.

"I even know why," he said.

"Tell me."

"Perhaps you've been living the way Kate does," he said, "but not the way Kate can do it. To Kate nothing much matters."

"I have not lived the way Kate does," she said.

"Then why did you offer?"

She shrugged and looked away.

"Ramon doesn't matter here," said Port. "I told you that."

"I raised him." She gave her short laugh again and said, "He is three years younger than I, but I raised him."

"No parents?"

"Oh yes. But they always worked. When they came to this country," she said, "all they ever did was work."

"He's grown up now," said Port. "You don't have to be your brother's keeper—"

Now she was angry again. She got up, stepped away from the table, and said, "How would you know?"

Port didn't answer, for his own reasons, and Shelly thought that it meant Port couldn't understand. For one moment it even felt as if she herself didn't understand any longer and it made her feel even more angry. She would let

Port sit and she would have nothing further to do with him. It was suddenly easy to dislike him.

She went back to her room and slammed the door. Port sat alone in the kitchen, and nothing felt right. He sat waiting for Ramon, impatient but without real interest.

When Ramon came in Port felt some relief. It would at least change the atmosphere.

"Sit down," he said. "You sure took your time getting here."

Shelly came out of her room. She was wearing the blanket robe, nodded at her brother, and crossed the kitchen to go into the bathroom. Ramon noticed that Shelly's legs were bare.

"All right," said Port, "tell me again about the calls yesterday. It's important."

Ramon turned around and tried to concentrate.

"Everything," said Port.

Ramon closed his eyes and recited. "First a call from McFarlane. In the evening—not the morning call. Bellamy asked why in hell he couldn't render a different interpretation of that special-group statute." Ramon looked up. "I'm sure he said special group, but I . . ."

"That's all right. I know what he meant."

Ramon closed his eyes again. "Next Bellamy called somebody called Pump on the phone. Pump or Sump. He only said the name once."

"He said Sump. Go on."

"This one he gave holy hell. He said it's an affront to the sensitivity . . ."

"Sensibility."

"All right, sensibility. He says it's an affront to that, the way the committee was handling the slum clearance thing, and then this Sump gives it back to Bellamy. Like a revival meeting, let me tell you."

"Just in brief, what did he say?"

"He said for Bellamy to go to hell. That's the way I figure it, anyway."

"What next?"

"Next, Bellamy makes a business call about some fine point about property. After that he talks to a man called Landis. This was very short, and . . ."

"What about that business call. Any details you remember?"

"Wait a minute. This Landis call, now, Bellamy tells

the man to stay out of politics or else, and Landis says, I am out. Out of your kind, anyway. Then Landis hangs up."

Ramon looked at Port, pleased with himself, but Port's reaction offended him.

"What about that business call?"

Ramon drummed his fingers a few times.

"You know, Dan, if you'd tell me what you're after, maybe I could listen better. I'd know what to listen for. You know what I mean?"

"You're doing fine."

At that moment Shelly came in. She went to the sink to do something or other, but most of all she interrupted. Before either of the men could say anything she went back to her room.

"All right, Ramon, what about that property? You remember the address?"

"I told you already. I told that mailman character. Twelve hundred Birch."

"That's right. What did Bellamy say?"

"Nothing. Just a question about escrow. I think he said, 'Is it in escrow,' or something like that."

"Whom did he talk to?"

"He called the man Jack. And Jack, all he said was 'Yes sir' and 'No sir'."

Port frowned and said, "Maybe there's something."

"How would I know? But if you'd tell me what this is all about—"

"Did he say, 'Yes, it's in escrow'?"

"Look, I don't know what escrow is and when they talked about it, it's just double talk to me."

"Double talk about what?"

"How in hell do I know!"

"Don't yell. You'll wake up your sister."

But Shelly opened her door right then and came back into the kitchen. "Are you all right, Nino?" she asked.

"Stop calling me Nino, will you? And don't keep busting in here like that when I'm talking business."

"I live here, Nino." She said it to Ramon, with a gentle voice, as if she thought he might have forgotten. She closed a cupboard door and went back to her room.

"Don't mind her, Ramon. She . . ."

"What do you mean, don't mind her? When I'm trying to do a job, especially something like this . . ."

"You're doing fine."

"I could do better, if I knew what in hell you're after."

"Let's get back to that call, Ramon." Port was patient. He would have to make the best of the situation, and he would have to remember not to come here again. Not to talk business, to mix business and pleasure— He almost laughed when he thought of the pleasure he'd had with Shelly.

"The Jack guy mentioned the Realty Improvement Company."

"Realty Improvement?"

"That's what I said."

"Did anyone mention Sun Property Management?"

"No. I'm sure nobody did."

Port leaned back, rubbing one hand through his hair. Ramon sat for a while, waiting, and then he asked, "Did I tell you something?"

"It sounds like they're selling. Sun Property owns the building and Realty Improvement is a broker. They handle sales."

"Maybe something crooked, seeing that Bellamy is in it."

Port shook his head. "Bellamy owns Realty Improvement, but that doesn't make it crooked. And if you want to sell property in this town, Realty Improvement is the best outfit to go to."

"So why the questions, if it's just one of Bellamy's legitimate business deals?"

"I don't know. Mostly because Bellamy's hoods turned up at that address. But that doesn't mean anything either, come to think of it."

"Would anyone like more coffee?" said Shelly. She came back into the kitchen and both men looked at her. She hadn't interrupted anything this time, so they just nodded and watched her pour from the pot.

She smiled at Port and said, "You want more, too, Danny?"

It surprised Port and it made Ramon frown.

"I only ask," she went on, "because you've been drinking the stuff over two hours." She had finished pouring and went back to the stove.

"Two hours?" said Ramon. "When did you get here?"

"He got here about twelve," said Shelly. She turned to walk back into her room and Ramon saw her bare knee where the robe came apart.

Ramon suddenly found that he couldn't look at Port. Two hours; so what? And besides, Ramon then remembered how he had thought that it might be a good thing if he brought Port and his sister together. But the thought gave him such pain now he felt the sweat come out of his palms like tiny needles and next only sharp rage could make it all good. Ramon looked up at Port, whose face was bland, who was blowing the steam off his coffee, who sat relaxed in his strength—and Ramon got depressed. He sank into a safe, heavy torpor, wishing only that he were asleep.

"What calls did you get tonight?" Port asked him. And then, "Hey, Ramon."

"Tonight?"

"Yeah. Anything tonight?"

It was important to be impersonal now. It would be easy. There was nothing quite so impersonal as talking about business—only it wasn't true. This, Ramon's job, was his life, could be the start for everything he'd never had.

"You get spells like that often?" said Port.

The light tone of voice helped, a tone that implied that Port didn't know what went on.

"Yes, several calls," said Ramon. "One call about a boxing contract, a long-distance call, and the man wanted to know if Bellamy meant to sell. Bellamy said he didn't know for sure, but . . ."

"Give me the next call."

"Next call. A man calls up to say Kirby was in the hospital, and they had to move out, and where should they go. He says a bastard by the name of Simon did it, and the big shot with him. He didn't say who this big shot is, but Bellamy seemed to know, from the way he started cursing."

Port started to laugh and then he asked, "Bellamy give any instructions to the man?"

"To go to hell, he told him. And to show up in his office in the morning."

"Okay, what next."

"A cultured guy calls up, long distance, and Bellamy is now doing the yes sir, no sir. I didn't catch the name, but he says 'Judge' to him. The judge gives a speech about ethics—no, about ethics of his office making the sale necessary, so that speed of sale rather than profit are essential."

"This is a business call?"

"Strictly. Because this judge apologized that he couldn't reach Bellamy at the office . . ."

"What office?"

"That's right! Realty Improvement! Bellamy is selling a piece of property for this guy, this judge, and the judge wants to know how it's going. And he wants no delays because of price quibbling."

"Did they sound like they knew each other?"

"No. They don't talk very long, anyway. After that call Bellamy talks to this Jack, you remember this Jack. He's a bookkeeper, it turns out, and Bellamy tells him to put the closing charges on the bill for Swinburn."

"What Swinburn, did he say?"

"Something about a motel. I think Swinburn owns it."

"That's right. South of town." Port got up, stretched his legs. "Any others?"

"That's all. Did you get something out of it?"

"I don't know yet, Ramon."

"What about this judge and Swinburn and all that?"

"Whatever it is, it sounds like legitimate business of Bellamy's real estate company."

Port paced back and forth, and Ramon gathered his courage.

"Dan, I would like to ask you something."

"Let me think for a minute."

But Ramon couldn't wait. "Dan, look, you gave me a job and I'm trying my best. Are you listening?"

Port nodded, looked at Ramon, and listened.

"But I think my best right now isn't good enough."

"You're doing . . ."

"No, let me finish. Would you say it's pretty important?"

"Yes, I'd say that."

"Then I think you should tell me what it's all about. If I'm going to do this thing right . . ."

"You know all you need to know."

"I don't think so. Unless I'm going to tap wire at Bellamy's for the rest of my life, and tell you about it like a parrot, it's not good enough."

"And," said Port, "you're not going to do that all your life. That's what you mean?"

"I figure I can grow in the organization. I figure with the way I'm working out, doing this job the way I am—" Ramon's courage failed him, and he stopped. He fought to find his way back, but for a moment nothing came.

"Go on, Ramon."

"I want in!" He bit his lip, but then it was too late. "I want in, I want to grow, and you're holding me up. I don't want to end up nowhere when this job ends up nowhere, because I got plans for myself! I don't think you're doing right by the job I'm doing, and you aren't doing right by me, if— After all, you picked me because I got something."

Port waited a moment, to give Ramon a fair chance to hear.

"You got something, and that's why I picked you. You're eager. And right from the start, Ramon, I told you not to get so eager that you get scared. You're scared of losing out. So you push. Don't push that hard, Ramon."

"Why not? You got one good reason why not?"

Port gave it up. He raised his arms, dropped them, and said, "You wouldn't believe me, Ramon."

"Just try me."

"All right: because it isn't worth it."

They looked at each other, and Port saw he had been right. He had said too much and Ramon couldn't understand.

"Worth it! Just look where it got you! You trying to tell me that it's worth staying a hick? You . . ."

"No. Not a hick. I didn't say that."

"You telling me you don't like what you're doing? Well, try me! I'll know what to do with it. I'd like to see those jerks snap to when I walk into the club, break up their daisy chain, tell them to run me an errand. What's more, I'd be good at it. I got the organization in mind just as much as myself. I can . . ."

"Right now you can shut up."

Ramon hadn't heard Port speak sharply before, and it startled him. But then he gave it the wrong label.

"Hold me back, will you? I'm not scared now, let me tell you, and while I'm at it, why don't you tell me the works, what I'm doing in Bellamy's basement? Maybe you're scared! Maybe if I know too much . . ."

"You almost got it, Ramon." Port's voice was just as sharp, but much lower. It gave the feel of a muscle tensing but it hadn't moved yet. "If they catch you, Ramon, with the wire down in your room, what'll they do? They'll twist your arm till you talk. Not so you can tell them how much it hurts, but to tell them all you know. How long do you think you'd last, not spilling, if you knew what I know and they're twisting your arm? Tell me! How long?"

Ramon sat down in his chair and his mouth came open.

"Simple enough?"

Ramon still didn't talk.

"Or didn't you know that kind of thing is part of the big position you're after?"

Ramon breathed hard, to kill his confusion.

"And following orders without knowing why, and getting the pants scared off you, like right now, that's part of the big career you got in mind. You got that clear now?"

Shelly had come back into the kitchen, and she stood by the door, not moving. Then Ramon thought he had the clincher.

"The way you talk, Dan, how come you stick around?"

"He likes it," said Shelly.

Port gave her a look that made her catch her breath. Then Port talked to Ramon.

"I'll tell you this much. After the Bellamy job you can stay in or bow out."

Just by chance, Port thought, Ramon might understand. But Shelly answered.

"He will," she said. "He'll bow out!"

Ramon whirled around as if stung, but didn't look at his sister for long. When he turned back to Port his face was livid.

"I'm in, and I stick! Nobody pushes me out!"

Port looked from one to the other, then he went to the door. "You know the score," he said. "Report to the mailman, like before."

After he had closed the door nobody spoke in the kitchen.

Chapter Thirteen

THAT MORNING the sun was very bright and the air fresh, making Port think of taking a walk. He took a few deep breaths and wondered why the town was so big, getting bigger all the time, but nobody minding the weather the way it was most of the time. A day like this happened only a few times a year. Then he noticed that Simon hadn't shown up. He grinned to himself and got his car.

After a short ride downtown, Port pulled up to the clothing store. The right side sold suits and ties and the left sold dresses and things for women. Port said, "Hello, Marv," to the man in the store and asked him if he might use the phone. "There's nobody in back," said Marv, and Port would be welcome.

Port sat in back where the small window looked out on a row of cans in the yard. He used the phone; nobody bothered him and he stayed there several hours. His calls had to do with 1200 Birch, with Swinburn's motel, with Realty Improvement Company, and with Sun Property Management. He didn't call Realty Improvement itself because he had no connections in Bellamy's office. His calls were to some local finance companies, to the recorder's office, and to the file room of the Real Estate Board.

It all turned out to make sense. Stoker could make of it what he wanted.

When he got to the Lee building office Stoker wasn't there, but Fries was. He took Port into Stoker's office, sat behind Stoker's desk, and said, "What have you got?"

"How come I'm talking to you?" said Port. "Where's Stoker?"

"Home in bed. While he's gone . . ."

"Something worse?"

"A few days in bed and he'll be back. In the meantime I handle the details."

Port sat down on the couch and put up one leg. Fries

had to shift to see Port, and it spoiled his pose. He had an idea Port had done this intentionally, but he kept it to himself and started to play with a pencil. He let it slide through his fingers so the point hit the loop of a paper clip on the desk. He kept doing that.

"I think you can take it from here," said Port. "I'll give you the details."

"You sound like you're leaving," said Fries.

Port looked at his fingernails and then up at the ceiling. "You can stop clowning, Fries. You know the same thing Stoker knows. I'm leaving when it's set up so Ward Nine stays together."

"I've heard you say it, but I don't know any such thing."

"So don't worry about it, Fries."

"I'm only worried about the important part. What did you set up?"

"The council will vote on the thing on Friday, next week. As far as I'm concerned it's in the bag. We should know what the vote will be a few days before. Like always."

"I don't know any such thing."

"Hell, Fries, you're supposed to take Stoker's place. Don't you know when the vote will be certain?"

"Stoker keeps track of that part."

"I thought you said . . ."

"He's got a phone, doesn't he? And besides, how come you don't know?"

"I've been doing other things."

"Any better than fixing McFarlane? Like you said yourself, his slum ruling will stand up just so long. If you're thinking of leaving when the council votes . . ."

"Fries, when somebody offers you a cigarette, I bet you say, 'Let's have the whole pack.' "

"I don't smoke."

The fine click when Fries dropped his pencil was getting on Port's nerves, but if Fries hadn't been doing that, something else would have gotten on Port's nerves. The thought made his irritation worse. He thought he was acting like Ramon, fishing for praise, and that didn't help. Then he made the mistake of trying to make Fries stop playing with the pencil. He said, "If you'll stop playing with your pencil a minute, Fries . . ."

"Why don't you come to the point," said Fries.

Port got up and came over to the desk. He kept his lips

shut tight because he didn't want to start whistling, and he didn't look at Fries, because he didn't want to lose his temper. He looked out the window and thought how nice the weather was, and how in a short while he wouldn't look at it any more, in this town.

"Here's what I found out, and then you can figure on how to use it. I think it's good enough to keep the ward almost indefinitely."

"Not counting the unforeseen," said Fries and dropped his pencil.

"Don't bother me."

"You might as well learn, Dan . . ."

Port reached over and grabbed the pencil out of Fries's hand and threw it down on the desk. "You want a clean deal on that ward job, or don't you? If you don't, I'll blow now and you can sew it up your way."

"I don't sew."

Port shut his eyes and groaned.

"Besides," said Fries, "you promised Stoker . . ."

"I got only one weakness," said Port; "one great self-destroying weakness. I let you get under my skin."

"I have hardly said a word, Port, and all you've said doesn't add up to a hell of a lot either." Fries had started to scratch at an inkspot, scratching at it with one long, horny nail.

"Here," and Port handed the pencil over. "Take your pencil, please. Just take it, click it, point it, and let me get out of here."

Fries colored, but kept still. Other people's irritations meant nothing to him, but a sharp voice made him apprehensive.

"Once more," said Port. He sat down, and went through the whole thing. "Like I told you and Stoker, they can't clear the slums, now that McFarlane ruled that it violates statutes. That can last a while, but not forever. What would hurt most is if they take it to the Capitol, and if I know Bellamy it'll be only a matter of time and he will."

"How do you know?"

"Fries, don't bother me, will you?" Then he went on while Fries sat and listened, though for a long time Fries didn't get the connection.

"The Supreme Court judge with the weight in this matter is Paternik. Paternik comes from this town, he's got the seniority, he's a figure. Did you know Paternik owns real estate here?" Fries waited. "There's an outfit in town, Sun Property Management. They don't just manage property, they also own some. It's a stock company, but the stock is family-owned. The name of the family is Evoy, but that doesn't mean a thing. It turns out they own the stock in the name of a relative, all very legal, and for no reasons of concealment. When you're rich, that's how you do it. Judge Paternik owns Sun Property Management, and that's how he owns Twelve hundred Birch."

"I see."

"You will. Right now the judge is trying to sell the property on Birch, because it is a blotch on his name. It's a substandard tenement in Ward Nine, and what with the stink about the slums, if it should come out that the judge owned property there—well, it's a stink."

"Paternik isn't in with Stoker," said Fries.

"So what? It doesn't look good. So here's your setup, Fries. Step in and put Paternik over a barrel."

There was silence for a while, because Fries didn't know what Port meant. Then he said, "I'll tell Stoker about it."

"You mean you don't know what I'm talking about."

Fries accidentally broke the point of his pencil, which meant he was much too busy to answer right away.

"Here's what you do, Fries. Buy the building from Paternik.

"Stoker has made it a policy—" Fries started, and was glad when Port interrupted.

"Stoker buys the building through a dummy, and he pays higher than valuation, way higher. Then if it's ever important to push the judge, you put it this way: Paternik sold something to Stoker—that's bad in itself. Paternik sold for more than the building's value. Is Stoker a jerk who pays more than something is worth? Not Stoker. Then what did the judge get the extra dough for? For services rendered. Judge Paternik in the pay of the Stoker mob!"

"I'll be damned!"

"You tell that to the judge once the sale has been made, and the judge jumps."

"He can show that the whole thing . . ."

"Don't use it till you need it. That's when you can ruin the man."

Port lit a cigarette and watched Fries get up. Fries took several steps, back and forth, and then he stopped in front of Port's chair. "Very nice. If it works. Get going on it."

"Run your own errands," said Port. He killed the cigarette without having smoked it. He got up and pushed Fries out of the way. When he got to the door he told Fries, "I sent Simon home. I won't need him any more."

Chapter Fourteen

PORT made a phone call from the lobby and talked to Stoker. "I just gave Fries all there was. He'll take it from there."

"What is it, Dan?"

"You got two setups now. The McFarlane ruling, to keep Council from voting against you. And if that doesn't hold there's a setup to keep the Supreme Court in line. Fries will give you the details."

Stoker smiled into the phone, thinking how glad he was that Port hadn't left.

"That ties up the bargain, Max. I'm through."

Stoker kept as calm as he could. He breathed deeply and let the first impulse go by. Then he said, "The vote isn't in, Danny. You promised . . ."

"What's the difference? How can they vote, except . . ."

"Danny. I'm in bed. I'll be up after the weekend. I won't have word on that vote till after next week's committee meeting. At least you can do me the courtesy to not take off at a time like this. Over the phone, me in bed—"

"When, next week?"

"The vote should be certain the day before council meets. That's next Thursday. Dan, you can make it easier for me and wait just those few days."

"I don't see what good it'll do, except to give you more time figuring out some new angle."

"Thursday night Bellamy's got an affair in his house. Political good-will meeting, he calls it. I want you to come with me."

"For display? So it looks like one happy family?"

"Do me the favor, Dan. All of downtown will be there, both parties. And some of the Capitol men."

"How come I didn't know about this?"

"Bellamy called me himself."

"Arranged from the top down. And plenty of press coverage at the last minute."

"How would I look, Danny, if you aren't along?"

A few days, so Stoker could look good in public, so Bellamy wouldn't smell the rift. It made sense, and Port thought of the delay as the last installment on paying a sick man.

"I'll be there," he said, and hung up before Stoker could thank him.

His impatience didn't catch up with him until he got out of the booth. The few days' delay suddenly became like a sentence. Port lit a cigarette, dragged too hard, felt the smoke tear a raw scratch down his throat. He coughed, making it worse. Nothing had shown while he had been busy. He had done his work with practiced speed, doing it well because Stoker needed it. He had taken Stoker's machine and for a few days of concentrated maneuvering had made it turn tricks. For Stoker, and for himself. For Stoker so he could keep his machine, for himself so he could get rid of it.

And now he was out. Nobody else might think so, but Port wanted to—except for a few, loose-end days in a town he didn't like, with faces he didn't want to see, and with a past riding his shoulder as long as he stayed. Maybe longer, except that once he was out it wouldn't be staring at him from quite so close.

Port walked to the parking lot and felt worse than he had in a long time. It upset him to find himself at the end but without the feel of conclusiveness. Stoker's damn party; Fries's damn threats; Shelly's damn attitude—Port got into his car, overtipped the attendant, and drove off too fast.

What if he were leaving today—what about Shelly? It occurred to him that he had never really thought of it, either because he had been too busy, or because— He yanked the car through a curve and then noticed where he was heading. A ten-minute drive and he'd be there. Then a few days with nothing to do but to concentrate. Shelly took concentration. With anyone else he might have thought of it like a sport, but not this time. This was a necessity.

He pulled up near the club, because most likely Shelly would be working the counter in the corner store.

She wasn't there. The grocer was working the counter himself and he didn't know where Shelly might be. Shelly had quit.

When Port got to the apartment nobody was there. He knocked, he tried the door, but nothing happened. He went downstairs again, reminding himself that there were, after all, several days left.

He walked half a block to the club, more out of habit than purpose, and stood in the archway to the room with the easy chairs. He watched the two guys tossing their ball back and forth and then Lantek dropped by. "There was a call for you. Maybe an hour ago."

"Who was it?"

"I don't know. Said she'd call again." Lantek looked at the clock in the hall. "At two. Ten minutes from now."

"You don't know who it was?"

"She didn't say. Sounded like a secretary."

Port couldn't place it, but then Lantek wouldn't know what a secretary sounded like.

"And the mailman was here," said Lantek. "He wrote something down and left it in the office."

Port frowned, because he had forgotten about the mailman. He didn't need him any more, but he shouldn't have forgotten.

They stood watching the ball go back and forth a few times and then Lantek said, "You seen Katie around?"

"No," said Port.

"We been kinda looking for her. She mostly don't stay away this long."

"Maybe she hit the jackpot someplace."

Lantek said, "Ha," and Port laughed too, but for a different reason.

He went to the office off the hall and got his letter out of the box. The mailman had listed three calls. One by Bellamy to McFarlane, urging the city solicitor to reverse his slum ruling. The answer was no, what was done was done. To that Bellamy had answered he'd take the matter as far as the Capitol—to the Supreme Court, if need be. McFarlane had answered that was perfectly proper and if Bellamy needed legal advice McFarlane's personal efforts would be at his disposal.

The next call had been to Stoker, inviting him to the good-will dinner next week. Port knew about that one. And the last call had been to Landis, with the same request, except Landis's answer had been that he would not be part of any more political farces.

Bellamy hadn't been very active that night. Only three

calls. He had started at nine and had finished at nine-thirty.

When Port tore up the paper to throw it into the waste-basket the phone rang. He didn't get there till the man assigned to the office had lifted the receiver and said, "Neighborhoodsocialclubwardnine." He listened for a moment and handed the phone to Port. "A very nice voice," he said and started to grin, but stopped it abruptly. Port nodded at him to blow and put the phone to his ear. "Port, speaking."

"One moment, Mr. Port. I have Mr. Bellamy on the line for you."

She *was* a secretary.

"Is that you, Dan?"

Port held the phone away from his ear.

"Yes, I can hear you."

"Look, boy, if you got a minute or so would you mind running out to my place? Just a talk, you and me. What do you say, boy?"

"You think you'll get any further than George and Kirby did?"

Bellamy roared with laughter and then said, "They didn't half try!"

"Bellamy, let me . . ."

"No, seriously, boy. Just you and me, for good all around. The good of the community, if you know what I mean. Now I'm at the office and could pick you up on my way out, except I don't think it would look right, me stopping over at your club. What do you say, boy? Half an hour?"

Port was quite certain Shelly wouldn't show up until evening. Job-hunting, probably, or working someplace else . . .

"I'll be there," said Port.

The place was as expansive as Bellamy himself. Port stopped on the rotunda in front of the house and tried to decide whether to go in at the Tudor entrance, the French Provincial one, or the screen door with the aluminum bird. A butler decided for him, showing up on the Italian terrace. Port followed him. Before leaving the terrace he saw Ramon in the distance. Ramon was raking a gravel walk that wound far across the side of a hill.

Bellamy was waiting beside a small frame to which a hooked rug was pinned. It was only half finished and Bellamy was fingering the needle. In his other hand he was holding a snifter half full of whisky, with a piece of ice in it.

"Sit down, boy, sit down!" He came across the Persian rug. Port and Bellamy shook hands, and Port wondered why some people insisted on trying to crush a man's hand, as if that proved something or other.

"Bollwick, bring Mr. Port—what'll you have, Port?"

"Rye."

"Bring him rye, Bollwick. Port, I see you are looking at my daughter's hooked rug. Amazing, isn't it?"

Port nodded and wondered why Bellamy put out all the energy; there was enough noise from the bright pepper and salt suit, the green tartan vest, and—of course—argyle socks. Bellamy was big and whatever he wore showed a lot.

"Here's the rye," said Bellamy. He watched Port take a sip and stroked the thin yellow hairs over his scalp.

Port said, "What do you want?"

First Bellamy had to give a big laugh again, and then he leaned forward. "What are your plans, Danny?"

"I'm right now planning to hear you out. Very good rye."

"I thought you were leaving Stoker," said Bellamy.

"That's hearsay."

"Not that you're acting like it." Bellamy took a large swig and swallowed noisily. "What with all the snooping and swooping you been doing the last couple days."

Port grinned. "Pretty clever of me, huh?"

Bellamy closed his eyes and said with a voice that sounded oratorial, "I have only the greatest admiration for you, Daniel."

"You said that beautifully."

"I mean it. You're hot stuff."

Port nodded and sipped his drink.

"So how come you're hanging around a broken-down outfit like Stoker's?" Bellamy wanted to know.

"Because Stoker is a friend of mine."

"Oh, brother!" said Bellamy and took a big drink. Then he said, "Don't you like me, Daniel?"

"I think you stink."

Port was sorry he had said that because now came the laugh again. It lasted until Port thought Bellamy had an affliction. It turned into a terrible cough which made Bellamy's scalp red.

"Oh, brother!" said Bellamy again, and then he got up. "Come along, Danny. I want to show you something."

Port followed Bellamy through several rooms, through a hall, down some stairs, and after passing a Ping-pong table they walked around the furnace. Bellamy went through a door and waited for Port by the bed in the room.

"You know where it is?" said Bellamy.

"Huh?"

"Maybe you don't." Bellamy pushed the bed out of the way, kicked at the floorboard, and watched the earphone fall out. The wire attached to it was just long enough to reach up to a man lying on the bed.

"Oh, that," said Port. "I know about that."

"So do I."

"Since when?"

"Ever since you sent your bogus electrician to put it in."

Port leaned against the wall of the room and put his hands in his pockets. "You're lying, Bellamy. You didn't know till last night."

Bellamy sat down on the bed and made the ice cube spin in his glass. "How do you figure I'm lying?"

"Because of what you said on the phone during the last few days. And because yesterday you suddenly stopped."

"You're right. I'm lying."

"Now tell me something, Bellamy. How did you find out?"

Bellamy laughed and got up. "It's a funny story. Let's go back upstairs." They went back upstairs and Bellamy kept chuckling and talking, because it was the kind of story he would tell at the club. For many years he intended to tell that story at the club.

He'd been up there phoning, in his study, when he decided he might as well have some coffee. So he rang the house phone to the kitchen and told the girl there to bring it up. The maid came in after a while and when she put down the tray on his desk Bellamy thought, What the hell, this is for me. Direct type that he is, he makes a grab for the girl, and she wouldn't stand for it. She knocked his hand out of the way and tried to walk out. Not to be put upon, Bellamy jumped up fast as he could, and all in clean fun, you understand, tried a new tackle. She held still just long enough to grab for the phone, gave him the knee, and then threw the instrument at him. "Believe me," said Bellamy, "I let her go."

They sat down in the room where the half-finished rug was on the frame and Bellamy went on. "So I figure, the hell with her, or at least, the hell with her right now, and pick up the phone. There's nothing wrong with it, except the wire is torn out of the wall box. And there was that other one, that thin little wire that went right down to the basement. Some story, huh?"

"Some maid," said Port. "How come she sticks around here?"

"She's my daughter's maid, mostly, and she hasn't been here too long."

"She won't be much longer, the way you described it."

Bellamy laughed himself out of the easy chair and went to the door. He opened it and yelled, "Bollwick, send in that new one!" He came back with a bottle from the small liquor cabinet and poured some into Port's glass. "Wait till you see her, Danny. Some girl."

The door opened and Shelly came in.

Port thought his collar was going to strangle him, and it seemed that the moment was never going to pass. She stood in the door, unable to move, because she didn't know what to do. Then Port got up, slowly, and solved it for her.

"How in hell did you get here?" he yelled.

"I don't have to tell you a thing!" She sounded just as loud as Port did.

After that came a silence. Bellamy clinked his ice back and forth. Then he said, "You two know each other?"

They both looked at him as if he didn't belong there, and Port stopped close to him on his way toward Shelly. "You son of a bitch," he said, but didn't wait for an answer. He took Shelly's arm and gave her a shake.

"Don't you know enough to . . ."

"Let go of my arm."

"And you get that damn uniform off and wait for me out in front."

"You'd like that, wouldn't you!"

"A damn sight better than that operetta outfit you're busting out of!"

"Daniel," said Bellamy. "You're talking to my help."

It distracted him. Port turned around, hoping that Bellamy would say just one more wrong thing.

"This isn't slave labor, you know. And my daughter did the hiring."

"She's unhired." He saw Shelly make a small move and snapped at her, "You shut up."

"The fact is," said Bellamy, "you better take her. I

didn't know about her brother being your man, when she got hired."

"She's not in on this," said Port.

"How do I know? Her brother recommended the girl when we needed a maid."

"Why in hell did you come here?" Port looked at Shelly. But she was too mad to answer.

"I'm sure," said Bellamy, "her brother had reasons, what with the neighborhood where she's been living. And not too far from that Neighborhood Frolic Club you run in that ward."

"Are you going to get out of that uniform, Shelly, or do I . . ."

"You better," said Bellamy, and because it hadn't been Port who had told her she walked out of the room without any more ado.

As soon as she was gone things were different. Port got his bearings back, he picked up his glass, and drank what was left there. Then he nodded at Bellamy and went to the door.

"Wait a minute, Daniel. We're not through yet."

Port waited.

"You didn't answer me, Daniel. I want you to switch over."

"You shoulda laughed right after that one," said Port, and opened the door.

"You come over and I won't touch your man," said Bellamy. "The gardener. Or did you think I was going to keep him on?"

"Go ahead and fire him."

"How do you think it's going to be between you and the girl friend, Daniel, when it turns out he doesn't show up any more. You make me mad enough, Port, and I sink him. She's going to like you for that?"

"What does he mean?" Shelly came running across the hall. She dropped her suitcase on the way and again said, "What does he mean?"

Port stopped her at the door and then looked at Bellamy. "He said he'd kill your brother, didn't you, Bellamy?"

The girl gasped and Bellamy's face got dark red with anger.

"She heard you, Bellamy. One witness too many."

Shelly yanked her arm to get free of Port. "You stand here and say that? You stand here and calmly discuss . . ."

"Yes!" Port was shouting. "He says it the same way you've learned to do it, the way you talked, that night in the kitchen. Remember? Like talking about some kind of merchandise," and he started walking across the hall, holding her arm.

"I can't leave," she tried to say, but Port cut her short. He kept pulling her.

"And he wouldn't do it any more than you would have, in the kitchen. Come on!"

On the way out he grabbed up her suitcase.

Chapter Fifteen

HE GOT HER into the car by force and slammed the door shut behind her. She sat there, not moving. Port thought she might try to get out again, but she didn't move. He got in at his side and drove off with a fast jolt. She said nothing till they shot out through Bellamy's gate. Then she turned on him.

"You swine, stop this car!"

"And pick up Nino?"

"Yes, and pick up Nino!"

"Because you've raised him and he needs you all the time? That's how good a job of raising you've done? That what you mean?"

The car gathered speed and went down the highway, away from the city. The wind made a furious racket along the shut windows. It matched the mood inside the car.

"Your clever mind," she hissed at him. "I hate it!" And then, "Where are you going?"

"I'm driving."

"Not with me!" and her hand shot out for the keys on the dashboard.

He slapped it out of the way.

"Sit still."

"I want Nino!"

"Aha! That's a different sound altogether. Now you've said it loud and clear. You'd feel better with Nino around, wouldn't you?"

"I said . . ."

"Safe and prim as hell, right? What is it, Shelly, afraid I'm going to rape you?"

"You know you can't! You know . . ."

"No. As long as there's you and Nino I wouldn't think of it. You're not even here! And all you ever feel is sisterly love, isn't it?"

She sat still, and Port started to think she was going to let it pass, when she suddenly swung out her arm and cracked the back of her hand into his face.

He jammed on the brake. At first he thought he was going to laugh but then felt himself getting furious.

"Stop the car," she said. She sat crouched in the seat, and she had one of her shoes in her hand, holding it so the heel made a hammer. Then she said again, "Stop the car and let me out!"

Port made a fast turn into a dirt lane and stopped the car. He was out before Shelly had found her balance.

The air was rainy and cool, with a strong leaf odor out of the woods next to the road, and while Port stood there, breathing it, he wondered whether she'd ever come out. Her teeth showed like an animal's, and when she stood in the road she stopped to kick off the other shoe and then didn't wait any longer. She didn't wait for him to move, but came at him.

He hadn't figured she was very strong or as determined as she turned out to be, but before he got the shoe out of her hand she had clipped him hard over the ear, had tried to knee him, and then bit his neck. He had to let go of her to get a good grip, and that's when he stopped fighting her off. He got a hold on her that changed the whole thing, except that Shelly wouldn't give in.

The next time she tried to knee him Port lost his temper. He picked her up, tossed her over the ditch, and was next to her when she jumped up. There was one heated look between them and then the front of her dress came apart in one loud rip. She froze, but Port wasn't through. He reached out and tore the rest she had on, and when she tried to free her arm to claw him, he yanked it all down.

He was holding her as if she might get away long after Shelly had no such thought.

He had taken his jacket off and Shelly was wearing it, and when she had reached for the cigarette he had lit for her she left the jacket the way it had fallen because they were still far out of town. Port was surprised to see how far they had come.

She said, "Your place or mine, Daniel?"

"Mine's more private."

"But mine is closer?"

"And I got better accommodations."

"Except my clothes are at home."

He shook his head sadly and kept on driving. . . .

"Mind you," she said, "it's no problem right now, but with no clothes how will I ever get out of here?"

Port said, "Huh?"

She rolled on her stomach and pulled the pillow out from under his head.

"I said, with no clothes, Daniel . . ."

"Yes. It's been on my mind something terrific."

She smiled down at him and then reached across to turn on the radio that stood by the side of the bed.

"It's a fact," he said. "You'll never get out of here. . . ."

The radio was still playing the next morning. Of course, there was nothing in the refrigerator. They held out till the afternoon, and then Port went shopping. He bought coffee, and steak, and lettuce, and eggs for breakfast. He forgot a number of things, including the bread, but they didn't notice that till the next day.

Port woke up from the sound of the shower and jumped up very quickly, but when he got to the bathroom Shelly was through already and wrapped in a towel.

She said, "Why, don't you always take your showers alone?" and laughed when he tried to grab her.

His shower was a disappointment to him, but he took it so fast Shelly was still wet when he came out again. . . .

She couldn't see him because it was dark in the room, but she knew he was looking at her.

"Are you awake?" he asked.

"For hours."

"Then why didn't you answer me before?"

"Did I have to?"

"Yes."

She came closer and put her arms around him.

"Ask me again."

"Will you come with me?"

He noticed that she was holding her breath, and when she exhaled she didn't say anything.

"Will you answer me?"

"I don't have to, Daniel. You know that."

Chapter Sixteen

HE BOUGHT HER some clothes which she wore just long enough to go out and buy herself something that fit. She took much longer than she had ever done in the past, because Port had told her to spend all he had given her. He waited for her in a hushed room with hushed salesladies and the clothes displayed ornamentally. There were no ashtrays, and Port felt uncomfortable.

After that they went out and had their first full meal in several days and finished with coffee. Port offered her a cigarette but she didn't want one.

"You look sleepy," he said.

"So would you be," she said. "You don't know what it's like, shopping."

He said, "Of course," and then they sat a while longer.

"I have to go now," said Port. "There's still some business."

It changed her mood. It showed even though she tried hiding it.

"A few days, Shelly, and it'll be over."

"Why not now, Daniel. What's a few days?"

"A promise."

"And then we leave?"

"For good, Shelly. Both of us."

She smiled at him and nodded. She took a mirror out of her bag and looked at her lipstick. Then she straightened her hair.

"I'm ready, Daniel. Drop me off at home."

"Look, Shelly," he started.

"I want to see Nino, to tell him that I'm leaving."

Port drove past the club on his way to her house and thought how often he had been in this street and how soon he wouldn't see it any more. And Shelly thought how she would never look at these streets again because she would pick up a few things, explain to her brother, and then leave for good.

After she had opened the door to the kitchen she and Port stood there a moment because they hadn't recognized Ramon.

He sat more bent than usual and when he turned he did it slowly. One side of his face was puffed and discolored, a white piece of tape covered part of his eye, and he carried one arm as if his shoulder was sore.

"Nino!" She ran to the table and stopped only when she saw how he was afraid she might touch him. "Nino! Can you talk? Will you tell me what . . ."

"I can talk," he said.

His voice was normal, and looking at him from a certain angle, even his face looked the same. But he had changed.

"You don't look surprised," he said to Port.

Port closed the door and came over.

"Like maybe you knew it all along," Ramon went on.

Port sat down and said, "Don't be an ass."

"Nino, will you please look at me. Nino, what happened?"

"You don't see Danny Port asking questions, do you, Shelly? He knows already."

Shelly looked at Port, and for a moment he was reminded of the way she used to look at him, here in the kitchen, not too many days ago.

"He got beat up," said Port. "By the Reform Party."

Shelly didn't act as if she had heard, as if it weren't important. She took off her coat, put it over a chair, and went to her brother. "Get up, Nino." She took him under the arms. "Nino. Can you get up?"

"Leave me be."

"You are going to lie down and sleep, if you can. Come to your room."

He came with her and lay down on the bed and Shelly took off his shoes. "Sleep now. I'll take care of you."

"Sure," he said. "Between you and him, over there . . ."

"Be quiet, Nino."

"And close my eyes? And turn the other way while you and that bastard . . ."

"Shut up, Ramon," Port said from the doorway.

"Shut up? I should keep quiet when nobody else does? You know what they said, what they asked me? They called

me a pimp!" Ramon screamed. "Whether I pimped for her
and what is Port paying! That's what they asked me, you
stinking bastard."

Ramon stopped, coughing badly, and when he turned on
his side to hide his face Shelly put out her hand and stroked
his hair. Port said nothing because he saw how Ramon felt.

"Nino, don't," she said. She said it several times, sooth-
ingly, and kept stroking his head.

After a while he turned around and sat up. He had
changed again, back to the cold, suspicious man they had
found in the kitchen.

"They were riding you," said Port. "You know what they
said isn't true."

"Do I? Where were you all this time?"

"I was with Daniel," said Shelly.

"You don't mean it!"

"I sleep with whom I like."

"Did you sleep good?"

Shelly drew back her hand and stood up, but didn't say
anything.

"Don't take it out on her," said Port. "I don't care how
bad you're hurt, Ramon, but don't take it out on her."

"You don't scare me any more, Port. I've had mine."

"I'm not trying to scare you, but don't talk like a pimp.
You're her brother."

Ramon didn't like it. "That's why I'm telling you, Port.
Get the hell out of here."

"What happened?" Port made a pause. "Did you talk?"

The whole thing came back to Ramon, the two men and
Bellamy waiting in the room in the basement. They had
started to beat him without explanation, and then Bellamy
had said to lay off for a minute. He had asked, "What did
you hear on the phone, what did you tell Port, what was he
after, what's he going to do, what'll he spring, what, what,
what," and each time they had hit him, in the same place,
each time in the same place till he thought his face would
burst open. He hadn't told them a thing.

He didn't know whether it was because he hadn't known
anything or because he was strong. The doubt made a
sore knot in his chest.

"What did you tell them, Ramon?"

"Nothing!"

"Would you have, if you had known anything?"

"Get out! Scram the hell outa here!"

Port sat down on the bed and took out his cigarettes. Then he asked Shelly to leave. She went to the kitchen and they could hear her at the stove.

"Something's eating you, and maybe I ought to know."

"Beat it."

"We're through?"

"I told you, Port, you don't scare me one bit."

Port took a deep breath, put a cigarette in his mouth, and offered one to Ramon. Ramon didn't take it.

"Maybe you don't remember, Nino . . ."

"Don't call me that."

"You're too mean not to be scared. But not of me. I never gave you cause, did I, Ramon?"

Ramon looked away.

"I even warned you not to get that way."

"So what? You warned me about getting beat up, too. That doesn't make me any less sore."

Port took a drag of his cigarette and watched the smoke disappear.

"I give you one more piece of advice. Get out of it, Ramon. You're not built for it."

Ramon laughed hard, even though it hurt his face.

"The boot? I did the job, and now I get the boot?"

"I think you're out already. Except not the way I meant."

"You know so much."

"I think you switched. You got in real deep this time, and switched to Bellamy."

"I did?"

"You'll find out, Ramon. It's no joke, if you stay."

"You buying me back?"

"There's a difference between you and me, kid—at least I know a mistake."

"You've had more experience."

"That's true, and a good reason why you should listen to me."

"Why don't you leave?" said Ramon. The good side of his face looked cocky, but the bad one looked soft and tired.

"I brought you some tea," said Shelly and put the tray next to the bed. She turned to look at Port. "Is he leaving with us?" And to Ramon, "You're coming with us?"

Ramon saw how Port's face got very still.

"I shouldn't have told him?" said Shelly.

"I don't know. He's in deep."

"Nino, what did you do?"

"Nothing. It's the same as before, except he's trying to make something of it. That Reform crowd is any worse than your outfit? Don't make me laugh, Port!"

"I wouldn't. They're both the same. Except you were working for me, not the Stoker outfit."

Ramon laughed good and hard this time, screwing his face around so it wouldn't hurt so much.

"Nino, answer me!"

"He joined up with Bellamy."

"Because he made sense! When I didn't crack he sat up, and then he made sense. About old man Stoker half dead, about you never giving a damn, about Fries who's a jerk from way back, and what Bellamy had to offer on the other side. I look out for myself, and that's all I go by."

"But Nino, it's no good. Daniel told me. And he asked you to come."

"I didn't hear any such thing," said Ramon. "All I know is he's got hold of you and he's lamming out."

"I said you made a mistake, Ramon, and maybe you can make it good. I don't want you along, but if you want out I'll give you a hand."

All Ramon heard was the part about Shelly. All he could think of was Shelly and Port and how it had all worked out for them, just as if he had planned it himself the way he had once wanted to plan it himself. And Bellamy had called him a pimp.

"It's not only that I'm staying," he said, "but so is Shelly."

Port got up and looked for a place to drop his cigarette. He dropped it out the window and came back to the bed. He took Shelly's arm and said, "Come along."

"I'm staying, Daniel. He's sick." When Port frowned she went on. "I'm not staying because of the way he talked, but because he needs me. You go home alone. Call for me when it's time."

Port smiled and hated himself. She hadn't meant what he had thought.

"Wear something nice," he said. "We got a party tonight."

He went to the door, but Ramon called him back.

"So you don't get it wrong, you bastard." He waited till

Port turned around. "Shelly stays here. Or maybe you don't get a chance to leave town at all."

If Shelly hadn't been there in the room Port would have marked up the other side of Ramon's face. He hunched his shoulders and tried to control his voice. "Bellamy told you that I never give a damn. You start fooling with me, Nino, and you'll learn different."

Nobody talked as he went out.

Port drove out of town because he felt like driving fast. He was preoccupied enough not to notice the car that was following him.

Chapter Seventeen

WHEN he did, Port was out on the empty highway.
Once a hay truck came driving the other way, but that
didn't slow Port or the car behind. Port couldn't shake it.
He felt in a bad enough temper without finding himself
being chased down a highway, and when the next bend
showed a roadhouse further down he stepped on the gas as
if he were going past. At the last safe minute he swerved
and skidded a black, ragged gutter into the gravel and
watched the other car shoot by on the highway. It came to
a stop when Port was out of his car and running through
the door of the roadhouse.

There was just the bartender, doubling as fry cook, and
a farmer who was drinking beer with his tuna fish sandwich. Port came around the bar before anyone realized
what he was doing and looked in the shelf space under the
cash register. There was nothing. There was no stick, no
billy, no nothing. The bartender came up, more surprised
than angry when Port slapped a bill down on the counter.
"Take it! Take it and move," he said and had the cash
drawer open just when the car outside made a long squeal
and stopped.

The gun was in the back of the drawer and Port skinned
his knuckles yanking it out. He made the other side of the
bar when the car doors slammed, and he sat down as if
waiting for a drink.

That's what it looked like to Bellamy, who pushed his two
hoods in ahead of him. He grinned at Port from the door
and watched one of the hoods go to sit on Port's right and
the other one on Port's left. When he saw Port whip out,
make a fat sound that snapped back his man's head and his
man flat on the floor with the well of red blood covering
the bad shape of the face. Port couldn't have watched all
that because when Bellamy looked back at him, Port was

sitting still, obscured by the other hood, and that one was dropping his gun to the floor.

"Pick it up, Bellamy."

Bellamy didn't see the gun Port was holding till he came around and stooped to the floor. The gun followed him down and then up again.

"Put it on the bar."

Bellamy did. He smiled at the bartender and then at the farmer in back. Neither of them had moved, and the farmer's sandwich was trembling in his hand.

"I'm going to ask these good people here," said Bellamy, "to back me up when I prefer charges. I'm sure that . . ."

"They don't want to be bothered," said Port. "The thing about bystanders, they much rather stay that way. Don't you, guys?" They didn't answer. "Especially when the fight's between hoods?"

This time the bartender nodded and the farmer pushed the sandwich into his mouth.

"With hoods," said Port, "a talking bystander gets it in the neck no matter which way he talks. You guys know that, don't you?"

They both nodded.

Bellamy shrugged and grinned to show what a good sport he was. "All right," he said. "I just want to talk to you, Danny."

"I'm not interested."

"You got a back room, bartender?"

The bartender nodded and went to the rear. Bellamy followed him, and after Port had told the hood with his arms up to pick up his buddy they all followed toward the back.

They stood around while the bartender was there. Then Port said, "You ought to order some drinks, Bellamy. Make it worth his while."

"Bring something," said Bellamy, who had lost his good humor. "Beer."

"Make mine rye. And a glass of water," said Port.

They waited around without talking while Port kept the gun in sight. The bartender came back with three beers and the whisky, and everybody took his off the tray. One beer was left because the man with the bloody face was still on the floor, breathing badly.

"You drink it," said Port. "Mr. Bellamy will pay you."

Bellamy did, and the bartender rushed out of the room, forgetting his tray and the extra beer.

"Before you start laughing and cutting up," said Port, "I want you to know what a filthy mood I'm in. I also got a date for nine tonight and have to change yet. All right?"

"My party?" said Bellamy.

"That's right."

"I don't want to see you there. I want you to lay low for a while, for your own good."

"What's in it for you?"

Bellamy hadn't tried joking once, and the sight of Port's gun nettled him. It made him very direct, without the usual mannerisms. "I'm taking this town sooner or later, and I want you to switch."

"I knew the last part."

"I know how you feel about it. You told me. Now I'm telling you. There's a little thing comes out in the afternoon paper about Daniel Port, Stoker's right-hand man, defecting in the interest of civic advancement and the Reform. It means you don't show up at the party tonight to make a display of yourself with Stoker, and it means you better lie low while the Stoker bunch cools off after reading the news. That's why I'm here. I got a place all set up for you . . ."

"When's that paper come out, Bellamy?"

"Don't worry about that part. I'm through horsing around with you, because once I decide . . ."

"Who's the animal?" said Port, and pointed at the hood who was sipping his beer.

"Now you listen to me, Port . . ."

"What's his name?"

"My name's Sherman," said the hood.

"All right, Sherman, finish your beer."

The hood finished his beer and then looked from one to the other.

"Now turn around, Sherman."

"Don't listen to him!" yelled Bellamy. "I'll see to it that . . ."

"It's my skin," said Sherman, and turned around.

He closed his eyes, waiting for Port to hit him, which Port did. Sherman fell down. Bellamy had to jump out of the way.

"You'll regret this! I'm going to make it my business . . ."

when Port raked the gun barrel down Bellamy's front, making all the buttons on the tattersall vest bust open.

"Get on the phone," said Port.

"If you think strong-arming me is going . . ."

"I know it will," said Port, and hit Bellamy under the heart.

"You got a gun—you wouldn't dare act like this—"

Bellamy went to the phone on the desk in the corner, walking crouched over because of the pain in his middle.

"Now call up that paper."

"It's too late. They printed hours ago."

"But they don't hit the streets till six. Call up and cancel the thing."

Bellamy laughed, for real this time, and called up the paper. He asked for the editor-in-chief, whom he called by his first name, and started out, "Look, Billy, this is stupid, but I'm supposed to tell you to keep your edition off the streets. It's too late, isn't it, Billy?"

Port held the gun in Bellamy's back and took the phone out of his hand. When he had the receiver at his ear he heard the editor's laughter.

"This is Port speaking. Daniel Port."

The laughing stopped.

"You know whom you're listening to?"

"I do. Yes, sir, I do."

"And now I want you to listen to Bellamy."

Port held the phone to Bellamy's face and then did a painful thing with the gun barrel in Bellamy's back. The raw sound which Bellamy made into the phone was impressive.

"That was Bellamy," said Port. "He's now going to . . ."

"Duress!" Bellamy yelled into the phone. "I'm under duress!"

Port listened for something from the other end, but the editor had nothing to say. Only his breathing was audible.

"Bellamy is right," said Port after a while. "And it's not the kind of duress you would want on your conscience. Here's your buddy again."

Port gave the phone back to Bellamy, who could hardly talk.

"Do like he says, Billy. I don't care what it costs, do what he says!"

"And tell him I'm going to cripple you if he doesn't," said Port.

"Yes, you heard right, Billy. Do just what he said."

"And tell him you're a vindictive man, especially from a wheel chair."

"Billy, promise!"

Billy promised, and Bellamy hung up. He was bathed in sweat and when Port stepped back, Bellamy sank into the chair that stood by the desk. He groaned and didn't know whether to sit up straight or double over. Port sat down too and smoked a cigarette to give the man time to recover.

"I didn't know you were vicious," said Bellamy after a while.

"Push me hard enough and I'm all manner of things."

"I can use you," said Bellamy.

"No you couldn't."

"I pay. I can pay you . . ."

"I don't do it for pay, only for necessity."

"Give it any name you want, Port."

"And I can also go without sleep for seventy-two hours, but not if I can help it."

Port went over to the two hoods on the floor, and saw that they were good the way they were for a while longer. He told Bellamy to get up, they were leaving, and followed him out to the room with the bar. Bellamy waited at the door while Port stopped to give the gun back to the bartender. "And there's two in the back room," he said. "On the floor."

The bartender stared, reached for the gun automatically. "I—I don't get it. I got nothing but blanks in this thing!"

Port held on to the bar for a minute, to feel the pressure under his palms and to think of nothing else.

"I was afraid to tell you before, but the gun . . ."

"Will you keep your voice down, for God's sake!"

The bartender swallowed what he had meant to say, but his expression didn't change.

"About those two in the back—how did you, what did you—"

"I scared them to death," said Port. "The way you just did me."

He followed Bellamy out of the door.

Chapter Eighteen

IT WAS getting dark when they got to Port's apartment. He shaved and changed but didn't take a shower because Bellamy was no longer wrapped up enough to be left alone for that long. He sat in a chair watching Port. Bellamy thought he could kill him—which would be a mess for sure; or he could force Stoker to break with him, which might even the balance. And in each case he would lose Port. How valuable is one man? If he let the man go, it would be like never having tried; if he just made him bleed, Port would come back to him; if he had him killed—Bellamy found himself back at the beginning and not one step closer to the right solution. He knew only that he hadn't solved it, and the thought wouldn't leave him alone.

Port took Bellamy to Ward Nine and when he picked up Shelly he even took him upstairs. Shelly's smile dropped off fast when she saw him, making Bellamy take a short step back.

"He came to drive us," said Port, "so me and you can sit in the back." They grinned at each other and Bellamy went down the stairs ahead of them. Ramon didn't show up. He had stayed in bed, smoking.

Bellamy's driveway had two entrances and there were two policemen at each. They had nothing to do but stand there, tip their hats regardless of which party affiliation drove through, and at the end of the evening there was an envelope waiting for them in the kitchen. The two at the entrance gate were kept busy saluting and waving the cars through to avoid a traffic problem, while the two at the exit gate just stood around, bored with each other. Every so often one of them took off for the kitchen, the old one for beer and little caviar canapes, the younger one to drink coffee and watch the maids. At the house another uniform waited. This one had been hired from one of the clubs, epauletted and braided like a South American

115

general. He opened car doors and helped riders get to the curb safely, and then he blew his whistle to make the chauffeur drive on. Port and Shelly stood by the curb and waited for the general to blow his whistle, except this time he didn't know what to do.

"Tell Mr. Bellamy to park the car," said Port. "And tell him we'll wait for him here."

The general did that. After the car had torn off to the parking area the general came back to the curb. "He says not to wait for him. He says he'll meet you inside."

Port and Shelly went up the stairs, laughing, but they would have been sorry had they known what they missed. When Bellamy tried to sneak into a side entrance he got stopped by one of the exit cops who was just on his way back from the kitchen. Bellamy's evil mood, his torn vest, and his haste in general meant a long delay while the cop decided to check with some guests whether it was all right to let Bellamy in. It made a spectacle which left the main hall deserted, except for Bellamy's daughter, who was doing the hostessing. Even the butler had left.

Janice Bellamy had her father's light hair and reddish complexion, but where he was heavy she was dry and thin. She looked up when Port and Shelly came in and said, "Mr. Port!"

"Miss Bellamy. May I present Miss Ramon."

Miss Bellamy stared, being short-sighted but without glasses on gala occasions, and when she recognized Shelly she just managed to say, "How unusual—"

Shelly smiled at her and made the mistake of slipping her cape off her shoulders. It showed the long evening dress which was designed to make broad lights over the hips and to reveal the bareness on top.

"Well," said Miss Bellamy. "It looks positively new."

"It is."

"Did Mr. Port buy it for you?"

"I gave her the money," said Port.

"I couldn't have swung it, on a maid's salary," said Shelly.

"I know that," said Miss Bellamy. "But I'm sure you know how to make out in spite of having lost your legitimate job."

Port took the cape from Shelly. "We'll join the guests," he said. "Will we see you after you're through here?" and he handed the cape to Miss Bellamy.

Port and Shelly walked into the room with the guests.

Because of the commotion that Bellamy had caused, almost everyone was at one end of the room. Port recognized several people but didn't see Stoker. He saw Fries, though, who was standing at this end of the room, fingering the half-finished hooked rug on the frame. He looked up and came over.

"Where've you been anyway? I thought you told Stoker to . . .".

"I couldn't make it in time. Besides, I had to pick up Shelly. Mr. Fries," he introduced, "Miss Ramon."

But Fries didn't unbend.

"Isn't she the sister of that Ramon who got thrown out of the club?"

"It's worse than that, Fries. He's a Bellamy man."

Fries wasn't going to be party-spirited, so Port and Shelly left him to the hooked rug. Then Port saw Stoker.

"Shelly, I'll leave you here. You want me to bring you a drink?"

"Just tell the man with the tray. I'll wait for you here." She sat down on a couch.

Port waved at the waiter and left Shelly.

Stoker looked old. He seemed to have lost more weight and his face was pale. He acted animated enough but the tiredness showed. When he saw Port he stopped talking. A low-key color came into his face.

"Hi, Stoker. Ready to make the rounds?"

"Where in hell you been?"

"I wouldn't run out on you, Max. Come on, let's circulate."

They walked, said hello here and there, looking casual.

"After the way you been acting, and no word from you for the past few days . . ."

"I didn't feel like answering the telephone."

Stoker looked up.

"How'd you know I called? You been home?"

"Most of the time." Port noded and said, "Hello, Mc-Farlane."

"Don't overdo it," said Stoker.

"Hello, Sump."

Stoker said hello too, but kept on walking. Port held Stoker's arm.

"Aren't you talking to him?"

"What for?"

"What for? Listen, Max, I came here for one reason only."

"He doesn't know a thing, if you mean the vote."

"He heads the committee. He ought to know what . . ."

"I won't know till ten. They're having a meeting and after that Ekstain will call here."

Port looked at his watch and saw it would be another half an hour.

"Half an hour isn't going to kill you," said Stoker.

"Just don't be so offhand about it."

"I know why you're here. We'll talk about it after ten."

Port didn't answer. He didn't feel like talking about it now, or half an hour later. He would sit out his promised duty, he would stick close to Stoker, for the show, but he had said his good-byes. Port looked for Shelly, and saw she wasn't alone any more. Two old men were on either side of her, acting like billy goats, and three middle-aged ones stood close by, each telling a joke but all at the same time. Shelly smiled and nodded, and tried to lean out of the way.

"I see Paternik," said Port. "Did you say hello to him yet?"

"We shook hands."

"How'd that real estate thing go? Did you try it?"

"I told Fries to handle it. I haven't asked him since."

"You want to keep track of him, Max. Not like you been handling me."

Stoker gave Port a sour look. He nodded a few hellos, shook his head at a waiter who was carrying a tray, and kept walking. It wasn't a very festive mood, thought Port, not the way Stoker acted.

"Did you see our host?" he asked.

"I saw him come in."

"Max, you're not laughing and smiling. I'm here so we'll look friendly together, and when it comes to Bellamy that should really amuse you."

"I barely caught a glimpse," said Stoker. "There was something about the policeman not wanting to let him in."

"And his clothes all mussed. Wasn't that funny?"

"How do you know? You just got in."

"I brought him."

Port thought it would give Stoker a laugh and told him how the day had gone, about Bellamy, his two apes, and the paper. Port didn't like Stoker's mood and tried to put things in a funny way, tried to make light of an evening which he meant to be his and Stoker's last together.

"I don't think it's funny," said Stoker. "When a guy like Bellamy gets that anxious . . ."

"He's bluffing," said Port, not believing it.

"Watch him, no matter what you do."

"You sound like a speech, Max. Come, I'll show you something nice," and Port took Stoker to the couch where Shelly was sitting.

She got up when she saw Port and so did the two old men sitting next to her.

"I'd like you to meet Mr. Stoker," said Port. "The old man himself, and my guardian angel."

They all laughed and then Shelly said, "And this is Judge Paternik and his clerk, Mr.—"

"Auburn," said the clerk. He was as old and impressive looking as Judge Paternik, but Paternik had something special. Nobody looked at the clerk any more while Judge Paternik started to crackle with magnetism.

"Mr. Stoker," he said, "and Mr. Port. I know both of you by reputation and welcome this chance, this non-partisan chance, to meet both of you man to man."

"We're delighted," said Port. "And I hope your presence, your non-partisan presence, will serve to temper . . ."

The judge couldn't have been listening because he interrupted to say, "Why, when it comes down to it, gentlemen, we all are, are we not, of the same . . ."

"You put it well, Judge, and I'm glad you did. Shelly, has the judge . . ."

"I have that, I indeed have that," said the judge, and under the guise of paternal affection he patted Shelly's bare arm.

"While I introduce Miss Ramon to our host, I'll leave you and Mr. Stoker together," said Port. He saw Stoker unbend and get affable, because the party was, after all, business.

"Why do we have to meet Bellamy again?" said Shelly. She held on to Port's arm and pushed herself close.

"Just to make it polite," said Port. "After all, he got dressed for us."

His tuxedo jacket—it went without saying—was Scotch plaid, and so was the cummerbund. In his haste he had grabbed a pair of pants with a plaid stripe down the side that didn't quite match the jacket. When they reached Bellamy, Shelly was happy to see there wasn't going to be much conversation. They passed each other, nodded with smiles, and Bellamy was gone. Port had not seen Bellamy being short before, not in public.

"I see the terrace," said Shelly and steered Port by the arm.

They went outside and leaned against the stone railing. They smoked and were glad to be together.

"It's over soon?" said Shelly.

"Tonight."

"And nobody knows?"

"Stoker does, but he won't believe it."

"I believe you. I believe you without your explaining it, just seeing how different you are from those—" She nodded towards the house.

"They're not that different from anyone else."

"But they think so."

"Let them. It makes them easier to spot."

Port looked into the lighted room and saw the rat race in operation. The false smile, the innuendo, the threat by ommission, and the dirty jokes and the club-house bravado, all making a hail-fellow-well-met gesturing out of the knife in the back.

Port saw Paternik standing alone, looking for the waiter who went around with the tray. Stoker had left him. Stoker was not in the room.

"Okay, honey—"

"You're leaving?"

"Once more. Have a chat with Mr. Auburn, to be completely safe."

She gave him a smile and they went inside. Shelly went one way and Port went toward the half-finished hooked rug where Fries was standing.

"Stoker get his phone call?" asked Port.

"Sure. You anxious?"

"Is he still on the phone?"

"He hasn't come back yet," said Fries.

They stood by the hooked rug and Port caught himself counting stitches.

When Stoker came in he looked subdued and had a flush on his face. He saw Port and Fries and came toward them casually.

"Well? What did you hear?" Port asked.

"You don't sound like you got much confidence in your setups no more," said Fries.

Port ignored it and waited for Stoker to speak.

"The Ward stays," said Stoker. "They're voting it our way."

Port found that his excitement had been artificial. He heard the words—meaning it's now all over—but there was no relief. Or the excitement was genuine but it had nothing to do with the news on the vote. He knew what the vote was going to be; he had known it for days. He thought he had known that with the vote in the bag it was over, and now he knew that it wasn't. Stoker put it into words for him.

"Danny, now comes the serious part. Come along."

He followed Stoker out of the room, and decided to make the break final. For the moment he didn't remember that he used to think he had done so before.

Chapter Nineteen

ALL RIGHT," said Port. "Don't act like a wake."

But Stoker didn't say anything, and Fries just closed the door. The room was long, with a sunken effect, and a sandstone fireplace designed for a bigger room. Stoker walked back and forth for a while, looking out the window, looking into the fireplace. Port didn't press him. This time, for the last time, let Stoker pour his heart out, tell of the old times and how far they had come, and the big things in the future as long as the team held together. Port wouldn't pay any attention to Fries, because Fries and his two cents' worth of wise comments weren't going to get in the way at a time like this. Port would concentrate on the appeal in Stoker's voice, his paternal pleading, and having heard it all before would let it come and go like a recital.

"Danny," said Stoker, "maybe you've made up your mind. If you have, maybe it'll kill you."

Port didn't talk, didn't even whistle. He watched Stoker stand by the fireplace, one foot on the sandstone apron, and the way Stoker looked it didn't fit the old image at all.

"I'm not arguing any more," said Stoker. "Pardon the phrase, but it's now bigger than you and me."

Maybe a joke right now. Maybe a little chuckle right here where the silence was thickest, and Port wouldn't feel so pushed any more. He couldn't make up his mind fast enough, because Stoker went on.

"You're a hood, Port. What's worse, you're a hood in the know."

Port narrowed his eyes, and this time he did start to whistle. It was as tuneless as ever, as offhand as all the times when he'd heard himself do it, except he was thinking how false it rang. If he were alone, he'd be screaming right now.

Stoker kept watching him.

"Why don't I trust you? You don't have to ask. I trust

you, but that's neither here nor there. One day I'm going to be dead. Before you, most likely."

Now maybe he'd revert to type and start with the old-times'-sake sermon. Port sat down in a leather chair, closed his eyes, and listened to the pillow sigh.

"Maybe even Fries trusts you." Stoker paused for a moment. "You know more than Fries does, did you know that?"

Port looked up at the ceiling.

"About our hookup," Stoker went on, "about the ins and outs of all kinds of traffic, how our little setup—our vote insurance setup—is just one of the cogs in the whole scheme, the whole balanced scheme."

Port chewed his lip and wondered how he might feel five minutes from now.

"That's how smart you are. In fact, sometimes I wonder, Danny, why you haven't moved up out of this setup." Suddenly Stoker changed his voice. "But you're not smart enough to walk out!"

The five minutes hadn't passed, but Port felt the change, the clarity come back into his feeling, and if he didn't quite know what he ought to do, at least the dullness was gone, the cottony vagueness which hangs, waiting, just before the fright sets in.

"You listening, Port?"

Port looked at Fries and then at Stoker. Either of them could have said it, and neither of them would understand his answer.

"I make sense," Stoker said. "Don't I?"

"Sure. Your kind of sense."

"What's that supposed to mean?" Fries wanted to know. Port got out of the chair. Not too much later he'd be walking out.

"It means that you and I don't think the same way."

"How come? You're maybe some kind of superior species?" Fries said.

Port turned away from Fries so the impulse to answer him would go away.

"Max, tell him to leave, will you?"

"Wait in the other room," said Stoker.

"By the hooked rug," said Port.

Fries was at the door with not enough time to think of a comeback. He closed the door behind him and the silence in the room started to grow again.

Abruptly Port said, "It all adds up to the same thing. I'm leaving."

He said it calmly, clearly, but Stoker did not want to listen. He talked as if he had not been interrupted.

"Here's your choice. It's either you or Fries."

"What?"

"Face the facts, Danny. I won't be here much longer. Which way do you want it: With Fries under you, or you under Fries?"

Port felt the rage grow, and he couldn't stop it this time.

"To me, that's not even a choice."

"There's another one. The one I told you at first."

Stoker saw the color come into Port's face, a thing he had never seen, and like an infection he felt his own face become glutted with blood, the heartpound loud in his ears, and he shouted, "Take it or leave it! I'm through begging you! Take it or leave it, and I don't give one stinking damn!"

Port's voice came out hoarse. He controlled its strength but no longer anything else.

"You go to hell!"

"Wha—"

"If I can't get rid of you and the air you breathe, you and the Frieses and Bellamys and the big shots with small heads and the small shots with big heads, then I'd sooner crap out!"

"I'll see you will!"

"Try it, Stoker. Try stopping me now!"

Port saw Stoker stare, breathing hard, his face ugly with great drops of sweat, and then he swiveled fast because of the sound.

But the door was closing already. When Paternik saw that Port was looking at him he went back half a step, smiled softly, and said, "I apologize. I heard voices. You will forgive an old man's curiosity . . ."

"Sure. That's all right—"

Port saw Paternik stand there, and then he came closer.

"Forget it," said Port, but Paternik didn't hear. Port could tell by his face. He wasn't even looking at Port. He was cocking his white-haired head, frowning, and seemed to be on the point of clearing his throat. He made a smooth movement closing the door, and when he spoke it came suddenly.

"For heaven's sake!"

Then Port heard what the judge was seeing, a thin, sick groan that cut off as if choked. A choke which was pain itself, pain freezing all motion to death.

It was a miracle that Stoker still stood. He did not even weave. His arms were out, a pathetic gesture of a hug interrupted, and the worn face was full of struggle. But nothing moved.

He collapsed suddenly, one leg still on the stone apron, and if it hadn't been for the sound on the stone, Stoker's falling to lie stretched out would have been a relief. The face was past tiredness and the arms were through trying to reach.

Chapter Twenty

THE PARTY broke up very quickly. Port didn't see anyone leave, but he heard the murmuring and the awed tones through the door, as if Stoker were suddenly somebody else and all the old relationships had died with him.

Before everyone left, and right after the cops from the gates had come into the house, Port had paid one of them to take Shelly home. Once Shelly was out of the house, Port went back to the room.

In the room with the dead man there were Port and Judge Paternik; Bellamy, who was the host, and Fries, who now had position. Fries left after a while because he had a lot to do elsewhere. They sat in the room with dead Stoker, one of the cops from the gate guarding the door.

"Not to distract from the tragedy," said Judge Paternik, "but it was fortunate that I came in."

Port smoked silently and Bellamy, who had his arms on his knees, looked up with a wrinkled forehead. He licked his lower lip once, then looked down again. His forehead stayed creased.

"I speak from the legal point of view. My entrance made me a witness."

"Not that it needed one," said Bellamy.

Port sat without thinking, waiting for the police, for the routine, but he was waiting for more. He hadn't reacted yet. He wondered whether it might have been easier to know how he felt if Stoker and he had finished their argument. Then, perhaps, it would all be clear now.

"Of course, when you say he had a heart condition," the judge was saying, "that makes the matter nothing but routine. Including the skull fracture."

"Is it fractured?" asked Bellamy.

"The sound was quite awful," said the judge.

Port remembered the sound. It had been like something mechanical, nothing alive. Port looked at Stoker as if he hadn't known until now that Stoker was dead.

126

It seemed to Port they had to wait quite a while. Off and on Bellamy and the judge exchanged a few words, and then Bellamy urged the judge to go home. There was no reason for him to stay, and a person in his position was certainly not required to go through the routine of police questioning. The judge thought the same.

"I can be reached at my home here in town," he told Port and Bellamy.

"I'll tell them," said Bellamy. "Maybe just a written statement, in case they bring it up."

"Of course," said the judge.

"I'll drop around," said Bellamy. "Just to see how you are and to give my respects to your wife."

"Mrs. Paternik stayed in the Capitol," said the judge. "Her activities rarely permit her . . ."

"That's wonderful," said Bellamy. "I admire that."

They all nodded at each other and the policeman at the door let the judge through.

When the detectives and the medical examiner came it turned out to be open-and-shut, and the inquest would be of the briefest kind. The detectives did all their duties, the lab men had just come along for the ride, and there would be a few more formalities later, nothing time-consuming, just the sort of thing requiring legal presence. It could even be done by mail.

It made a peculiar after-the-party feeling in the empty house, leaving no tensions and causing no stir.

"Want a drink before leaving?" said Bellamy.

"No thanks. I'll be going."

"Take your time," said Bellamy. "When it happens, it's always a surprise."

"Yeah. That's true."

"You don't know where to put your feelings."

Port didn't like to hear it from Bellamy, but it was true.

"Take your time. If you want a drink, you know where to find it," and Bellamy walked out of the room, leaving the door open.

Port got up too, but when he got to the hall it was empty. He had a hat somewhere. He found it on the hall table, only one hat left on the table, and then he went back to the room with the bar. He reached for a bottle to pour a drink, but then he stopped, wondering why he needed a drink because he suddenly found that his ties were gone.

He walked out of the house, closed the big door behind

him, and stood on the dim terrace. There was another light
further away, at the curve of the driveway, and it showed
the wet night fog hanging in the air. Port breathed deeply.

This was the time! He had thought his planning had
made him ready, his schemes, and then in the end, if nothing else, his decision. But Stoker had been alive, and
the sick man's invisible hold, stronger than threats, had
worked better than arguments, because leaving then had
still been a walking out. But not any more.

He ran down the stairs three at a time and kept running
till he got to his car. It wasn't a need to hurry, just the
feel in his muscles, in his lungs, of moving freely. He was
whistling when he drove off, loud and strong.

He wasn't going to wait till morning. He would pick up
Shelly in the middle of the night and they'd drive out of
town before the light came up. And if she were in bed, that
would only delay them long enough for her to get dressed.
But he was sorry—on the way to her house—that all the
florists were closed.

Shelly wasn't in.

There was a light in the kitchen, the door wasn't locked,
and Ramon was lying in bed. One side of his face was dark
purple, with a white, professional bandage higher up.

"Where's Shelly?"

Ramon was smoking and didn't answer. He took long,
steady drags and lay on the bed, dressed, without moving.

"You got a fever?"

"I'm all right."

"I asked you where Shelly is!"

Ramon dropped ashes into the cup by his bed and said,
"She's out."

Port sat down on the bed and didn't look at Ramon.

"Did she get home?"

Ramon was very casual—except for the strong hostile
streak under his voice.

"She got home. Then she went out."

"For medicine or something?"

"Yeah."

Port looked at his watch, then took out a cigarette. When
he had lit it he blew the smoke up in the air so it wouldn't
drift toward the sick man. Then he looked at Ramon.

"Why don't you lay off me. You'd make it that much
easier all around," Port asked.

"What makes you think I want to make it easier for you?"

"I don't know what, but I'm not in your way."

"I'm seeing to that," Ramon snapped.

"What more do you want? I'm leaving, and you're all set with Bellamy."

"I'm remembering that."

"And with the upset in the Stoker outfit right now, you made a good thing of it."

"That's what I'm working on."

"Do that. And leave me alone."

"I'll do that. When you stay away from my sister."

Port got up. "You're going to be a real big wheel. I can see that. You not only get excited about things you got nothing to do with, but you keep bucking the wrong people."

"You don't scare me," said Ramon.

Port gave him a tired look and walked toward the kitchen. He said, "I'll blame it on the fever," and sat down.

Port sat and waited. He could hear his own breathing and now and then the creaking of Ramon's bed, small sounds but heavy. The sound of someone moving in bed was always a heavy sound, as if the bed wouldn't let go. Then the feel of it spread to the kitchen and Port sat very still, feeling the weight grow in the room, and he didn't move because he was balancing it.

He had imagined this differently, his coming in, the first words, and then what Shelly would do. He was going to say, "Now, Shelly," and that's all he would have to say for her to know what came next—she would just go with him, and that would be their beginning.

Port wiped his hand across his mouth and went back into the room where Ramon was.

"I'm going home to get my bags," said Port. "When Shelly comes in tell her I'll pick her up."

"Like hell."

Port controlled himself, remembering that the man was sick.

"Just tell her."

"I'll tell *you* something," said Ramon. "I don't pimp for my sister."

Port could make out Ramon's face by the light from the kitchen, but with Ramon's face disfigured it was hard to tell what he felt at the moment. He hadn't sounded just tough, the way he must have meant it. Perhaps it was the pain and the fever. Mostly fever.

It was long after midnight, and Port made good time. When he got to the building he took the stairs up because it felt faster, and when he saw the light under his door he started to run. It explained Ramon's answers; he hadn't known where Shelly was. Port opened the door.

Chapter Twenty-one

NOW THAT you're here, close the door," said Bellamy. Port closed the door.

Kirby was there with a gun in his hand, and Judge Paternik was sitting on the bed.

"You can put the gun away, Kirby. He doesn't carry one," said Bellamy.

Kirby did, and then Port started to tremble.

"You might as well hear all of it, Port." Bellamy turned to the judge. "You want to tell him?"

"Perhaps you should ask him first," said the judge.

Bellamy shrugged. "Port, I've asked you often, I've asked you nice. You're staying in town, working for me."

There was a tight knot of hate inside Port's chest, and he held it there, sweating, till he could use it.

"No answer, Daniel?"

"Why don't you take a flying . . ."

"Shut up, you crazy hood!"

It felt very much like the mood in Ramon's kitchen, with the growing weight pressing down hard. There was something here, something very big, like the foreboding before a dream turns into a nightmare.

"I've got you dead to rights this time."

"What?" said Port, and he sounded hoarse.

"Judge?" and Bellamy raised his eyebrows.

"It was murder," said the judge.

Port felt his limp arms and very heavy hands. As a rational man he would not have believed this; he might even have laughed. But he wasn't that. He heard what the judge had said.

"I saw you do it, Port. I witnessed the crime, which I will detail to the police."

"Unless you join up," said Bellamy, but Port didn't hear him.

The judge said, "Why haven't I done so yet? Very

simple, Mr. Port. I too have a heart condition, and as a consequence of the murder I witnessed I could have stayed only upon jeopardy of my health."

"You're sewed up."

"Now, in detail," said the judge. "I walked in at the end of a quarrel—it was the shouting which had attracted my attention—and saw you deliver a powerful blow to the back of Stoker's head. I will say that having witnessed this, it is my opinion, no matter what the immediate cause of death, I feel that if this isn't murder, the law is a farce!"

Kirby half sat on the windowsill, arms folded, grinning. Bellamy sat hunched forward now, with his shoulders more massive because of his pose; and the judge sat upright and gave Port a clear glance. The white hair was as imposing as ever, the full eyebrows gave depth to his eyes, and the old mouth was in a settled line, not severe, but contained.

"Why—" said Port. He was looking at the judge. "Why you?"

"Didn't you know?" said Bellamy. "The judge heads up the Reform Party."

They gave it a chance to sink in. They watched Port open his mouth without making a sound, and when he closed it they felt he was done. Nothing showed in his face, nothing moved, only his hands started to rub up and down the sides of his pants.

"You see it now?" asked Bellamy.

Port saw nothing. He only felt that they could do anything, that they had everything, but he saw nothing. They had the powerful, big Bellamy, the name and brain of Paternik, gun-happy Kirby, big-dreaming Ramon—everything.

"Where is Shelly?" Port said.

Port didn't notice the way they frowned, not knowing what he wanted, but Port didn't follow it up. The tight knot of hate had started to loosen and grow, and the size of it grew over his head. It got so big for him that he couldn't stand it and it turned into panic. When he moved it was panic that pushed him.

He was out of the room fast and then out of the building. He didn't think of the men in the room and what they might do, about the distance to go, how long it might take him. He was back in the slums, with no knowledge of time and no change in pace. Only one thing had suddenly changed—his drive was no longer a crazy splatter of fear but a very sharp, pointed force. If he hadn't been out of breath he would have whistled now, but when he stood in Ramon's room he was very still.

"Where is she, Ramon?"

Ramon laughed.

Port stepped closer and the man in the bed was out of the shadow now, back in the dim light from the kitchen. Ramon was on his back, as before, and the gun in his hand was pointing at Port.

Port saw it, but it had no effect. His thinking was clear, his movements decisive, and he could hold them forever, to get his advantage.

"Bellamy's going to tear off your skin, Calvin, if you shoot me."

Ramon laughed again.

"He's the one that called you were coming, and said I should be expecting you."

"And to bring me back."

"Alive—if I can," Ramon said softly.

"Can you?"

"Any gun's bigger than you," said Ramon, and sat up in bed.

"That's why," said Port and before Ramon was properly settled the gun flew out of his hand with Port's sudden slap.

He didn't hit Ramon. He watched him get up, and then he spoke once more.

"Where is Shelly?"

Ramon stood stiff and afraid, with a fast spasm inside his stomach. When Port took a step forward Ramon said, "She is safe," and then he stopped.

Port wondered about Ramon's fear for his life and the stubborn answer. It was a part of Ramon he had never seen, and Port frowned.

"I tell you this because I'm afraid," said Ramon, "but I am not so afraid that I'd tell you more."

"Then I believe that she's safe."

For a very brief moment they were not enemies, but then Ramon cast down his eyes, as if the feeling shamed him, and Port stepped back to the wall to pick up the gun. Shelly was safe. There was time now for unfinished business.

"We're going to do like Bellamy wants it. Where's he waiting?"

"At your place."

When they got into the car, Port put the gun in his pocket and drove back the way he had come. He drove back just as fast but he knew why he was doing it now, and the wild excitement inside him was bright and hot.

They stopped at a building unfamiliar to Ramon, and when Port pressed the button downstairs there was only a number next to it. The buzzer sounded, and Port pushed Ramon ahead. The apartment door opened as soon as Port reached for the bell.

Fries had been in bed, but his thin hair was combed, he wore trousers, and the silk coat and ascot looked very correct.

"Let me in," said Port.

Fries wouldn't step aside.

"What do you want?"

"I'll tell you inside," said Port and pushed Fries out of the way. Ramon came in too.

Fries said, "What's he doing here? Isn't he the guy that got thrown out of the club? If you think for a minute . . ."

"Close the door, Fries." Port was going to the lighted room with the desk, and Ramon was following him.

Then Fries came in. "You're not starting out very well," he said, "now that Stoker is dead. From now on this free-wheeling stuff is out. I'm setting up regular hours . . ."

"This couldn't wait, Fries. Listen to me. Did you buy the Paternik building?"

Fries didn't seem to hear. He sat down at his desk and picked up one of the sharp pencils he kept there.

"Now then," he said.

"Twelve hundred Birch—did you buy it?"

Fries tapped the pencil on the desk and said, "What's it to you?"

"I need it! I need that frame for a trade, or Paternik will push me into a murder indictment. He was there when Stoker died."

"You murdered Stoker?"

"For Christ's sake, Fries!"

It would have been easy to grab Fries and choke the ascot around his neck. Port swallowed and lowered his voice.

"Yes or no, Fries. Did you set up the frame?"

The voice made Fries look up, and he saw the murder in Port's face, close to the surface.

"Yes," he said. "I did."

Port relaxed and started to smile. From now on it would just be one step after another to the end.

"Fries, you're a doll. Let me have the papers."

"What papers?"

"How much did Stoker pay extra for that property?"

"Twenty thousand."

"Receipted separately?"

"Of course."

"That's what I want. That receipt."

Fries pursed his lips and looked at his pencil.

"Or I'll break you."

Fries looked up, because his first thought was that Port meant it now. He couldn't tell what Port's exact meaning had been, and he had a thousand vague speculations. But the thing about Fries was his stiff, well-armored shell.

"You don't have to do that," he said. His insides were twisting, but all that showed was his remark. It carried him over the moment, and Port relaxed too.

"All right, I'm waiting."

Then Fries went on hastily. "What would you do afterwards—leave? You take the receipts and the organization can't use them any more. And on top of that, you blow."

Port felt something near boredom. He said, "If you don't give it to me I'm out of the organization just the same. He's framing a murder, I told you."

"It wouldn't stick. At best they can make it manslaughter. And with the weight we carry around here . . ."

"Give me the paper."

"And you stay."

Port looked away to reach for a chair and when Fries saw his face again, Port wore a small, vicious smile.

"I stay," said Port.

That made Fries sit up, his face very still, all the tics gone out of it. Then he heard Port go on, smiling.

"And when I stay, Fries, do you think you'll be the top man? Even Stoker told you, don't you remember, he even told you I know more than you do."

"Just a minute, Port . . ."

"I don't like you, Fries, and when I'm in, you're going to feel it. You understand that sort of thing, don't you, Fries?"

"If you think for a minute . . ." Fries stopped.

Port said, "Your kind of gutless creep never knows why

you can't make the top, with all your filthy scheming. I'll tell you why not, Fries: because all you ever know and all you can ever do is to kick up the dust so your tracks don't show, so your scared insides don't give you away, and the scream for help doesn't·bust out of you! I know that better than you, and that's why you can't win, not with me around, not as long as I run my business my way. I stay, Fries, and I'm going to ruin you! It wouldn't kill you, but you'd look a mess. Tell the truth, Fries, that's worse than anything, isn't it? That's worse than death to you."

Fries covered one side of his face, because his tic was now driving him crazy. He thought one eye might jump out or spit would drip out of his mouth.

"Give me the paper, Fries, and I'll blow."

There wasn't any more argument.

They drove to the Lee building and went up to the office where Stoker used to be. Fries went to the safe in the corner, and when he came back he had what Port wanted. Port took the paper. But for Fries there had now been enough time to collect himself; not that the words would matter too much, but he had to say it.

"You can't get away with it. If I want to . . ."

"But you won't, will you?" Port was smiling, which in a way was worse to Fries than shouting would have been.

Port took a sheaf of papers out of his pocket, folded typing paper which Fries saw was a carbon copy. Port laid it all down on the desk.

"Read it, Fries. And when you're through, you'll know as much as I do. About dirty politics, about our hookup, about payments to whom, and what law violations didn't get on the docket. With a lot of details about you and—more important—about men higher up. A criminal investigator's dream, big shot—and insurance for me."

"Where—where is the original?"

"Where will it be if I die?"

Fries waited.

"It'll be all over. So here's what you do with it, Fries. Pass it on to the top when you make your report about Daniel Port leaving the fold, and point out that it's safer that I stay alive."

Fries put the papers down. He would read them later.

"There are ways, Port. There are experts who make a death look like . . ."

"It says right at the bottom, Fries, this thing comes out

when I die. No matter how. That trick ought to impress you." Port started to laugh.

Fries tried to think of something else he could say now. "You can't—you can't—" he managed.

"Can't what?" Port was still smiling.

"Can't take the car! It's company property, if you come right down to it. Stoker just . . ."

Port's laughter was like a volley of slaps in the face, and when he threw some keys on the desk Fries grabbed them up as if they were his salvation.

"You'll like that, won't you, Fries? Those two big antennae in back, they really got to you, huh?"

Port waved at Ramon, who ran to open the door, and then they walked through the outer office. Port stopped at the switchboard and made three calls. One was for a taxi and with the other two Port used first names. Ramon didn't know what the calls meant.

Since losing his gun Ramon hadn't said a word, and Port hadn't tried talking to him. If he would talk, Ramon thought, maybe it would be like a sting which could arouse him again, make him find his old role, the one he had lost when they left the kitchen. The one he had lost when Port didn't beat an answer out of him. But they sat in the taxi and nobody talked.

Chapter Twenty-two

WHEN the taxi pulled up at Port's place, the prowl car was waiting. Ramon saw it first. He felt like crouching into the seat, hiding himself, and he was afraid Port might notice. But Port wasn't paying any attention.

One cop was on the sidewalk, the other one sat in the car.

"You better both come," said Port and ran into the building. He heard one of them say, "Yes, Mr. Port," and then Port tapped his foot nervously, waiting for the elevator to open. He pushed Ramon in first, then let the policemen pass by. On the way up he said, "You wait in the hall. When I'm ready for witnesses, I'll call you in."

"How many are there?" asked one of the cops.

"There's Bellamy. You know Bellamy."

The cops looked at each other and then Port went on, "And Judge Paternik. You've heard of him."

The elevator doors opened, so the cops didn't have a chance to look at each other.

They stopped in the corridor and Port said, "You can tell it's important. When you come in I want you to make an impression. Have your guns out."

They nodded without understanding and watched Port and Ramon walk to the door.

They were all there: Paternik at one end of the bed, Bellamy at the other, like balances on a scale. Kirby was on a chair, his gun looking at Port.

"What happened?" said Bellamy. His voice was loud, irritated, and he looked from Port to Ramon.

"Just stay by the door," said Port to Ramon, and stepped into the middle of the room.

"And you drop it," said Kirby.

Port shrugged, reached for the bulge in his pocket, and tossed Ramon's gun on the floor.

"I'll get to you later," Bellamy yelled at Ramon. "When I give an order . . ."

"He brought me, didn't he?" Port smiled.

"All right. Now you, Port. You've taken all the sweet time you're going to get . . ."

"Why don't you tell your dog to put down the gun. You know I don't carry any."

"He stays as he is!" roared Bellamy, and Kirby did.

If Port was impressed it didn't show. He went to the couch where his suitcase was. He did it so easily, without sudden movements, Kirby let him do it. Port opened the suitcase, took out a handkerchief, and blew his nose. They waited, with the tension thick in the air.

Port put the handkerchief back in the suitcase and when he straightened up he shot Kirby.

The man fell smoothly out of the chair. After a moment he slowly pulled up his legs and made low sounds. Port said to Ramon, "Stick your head out the door and tell them it's nothing. They should wait."

Ramon did it. Port tossed his gun up and down, waiting, and they all waited for Port. When the door was closed again he smiled at the judge.

"I'm back."

The judge frowned, cleared his throat, gave one quick look at Bellamy. But Bellamy wasn't helping.

"I'm here to trade murders," said Port.

There was a pause while Port let them catch up with the words. Then he said, "Paternik, did you ever sell that building?"

"I fail to see— The serious matter—" said the judge, not understanding.

"Paternik, listen to me. Twelve hundred Birch—you sold that, remember? And at what a price!"

"If you think stalling around with that gun in your hand . . ."

"Shut up, Bellamy."

Bellamy's face got mottled but he didn't move.

"You sold it to Stoker," said Port. "You know what that means, Paternik?"

"Port, what are you saying?"

"That alone looks like collusion with gangsters. And now this!" and Port held out the receipt. "You got a price that has nothing to do with the property's value. You got paid extra. You know what that extra was for, Paternik?"

"You must be insane!"

Port smiled and waved the receipt back and forth.

"That's not how it's going to look after I get through making mud out of you. It's going to look like political murder!" Port smiled. "You and me, Paternik, are going to trade murders."

"For heaven's sake—"

Port went over to Kirby and looked down at the man. A wet stain was spreading high up on one leg.

"Tell them, Kirby. How's it feel?"

Kirby started to make little sounds, and they all heard.

"And this one," said Port to the judge; "he's going to be as good as new in a month or so. What'll you be doing, Judge Paternik, in a month or so?"

The old man got up, then sat down again. He looked at Bellamy, who hadn't said a word.

"I'm through waiting," said Port. "Call them in," and he nodded at Ramon.

The judge got up fast, talking urgently. "Mr. Port, you asked me to consider. You offered a bargain to which I —" That's when Bellamy moved. While the judge held Port's arm, talking to him, Bellamy charged to the end of the room where the guns were lying. It wasn't clear what he meant to accomplish, because had he tried shooting Port the judge would have been in the way, but it never came to that. The two cops came in, with guns, and one of them said, "You're under arrest. Assault with a deadly weapon."

The gun fell out of Bellamy's hand.

"And this one," said Port, "is Judge Paternik. He is . . ."

"Please! Mr. Port!"

"He is here to give us a statement. A straight witness statement, because he hasn't had a chance to tell the police about Stoker's death."

"Yes," said Paternik. "A mere formality. I was present when Stoker suffered his heart attack, and then fell on the stone apron at the fireplace. This young man and I saw it happen, and though I was present, witnessed the natural death, I have not had an opportunity to submit my statement. I welcome this chance . . ."

"That's enough," said Port. "Now get this one for breaking and entering."

"Okay," said one of the cops, and took Paternik by the arm. When he had him up to the door, he told Paternik to wait while he picked Kirby up from the floor.

"This will never stand up!" yelled Bellamy, and the cop

who was holding him said, "You should tell it to the judge."

The judge and Bellamy looked at each other like strangers. Port said, "It's good enough till tomorrow, right, officer?"

"Okay, Mr. Port." They started to leave.

"Wait a minute." Port came after them. He tapped the judge on the shoulder, smiled at him. "This is yours," he said, and gave him the twenty-thousand-dollar receipt.

When they had gone Port and Ramon left too. Ramon carried the two suitcases.

Landis opened the door himself. He had been waiting for over an hour but the hair standing up in back of his head and the shadows under his eyes made him look as if he had just come out of bed.

"I thought you were alone," Landis said.

"Ramon will wait in another room," Port answered, and Ramon left.

Landis took Port into the kitchen and asked him if he wanted coffee. Port said no, and Landis picked up his cup, leading the way to the study.

"I'm not used to being up at this hour, Port, so if you'll come to the point—"

Port waited till Landis sat down.

"You still got my airplane ticket?"

Landis put down his cup very carefully.

"I thought you were joking, the last time I saw you." Port shrugged.

"The fact is," said Landis, "I do have it."

"You can give it to me now."

Landis went to the desk and found the ticket. He gave it to Port. "And have a good trip," he said.

"Thank you, Landis."

Landis went back to his cup but did not sit down.

"You wouldn't consider staying?"

"No."

"You are simply leaving the mess."

Port gave a short laugh. "Yeah, it's that simple."

"I had thought, when you called me . . ."

"I called to leave you the mess."

Landis raised his eyebrows.

"You want it?" said Port.

Landis went to the desk, sat down, took a pencil and

moved a long pad into position. Port walked back and
forth in the room and while he talked Landis wrote it all
down.

When Landis got up he drank what was left of his
coffee, never noticing that it was cold. Then he said, "You
realize this implicates your organization as much as the
Bellamy group."

"I'm through here."

"Yes. I see that. May I ask how you expect to survive
this kind of exposure?"

"What I gave you is local. Nothing else."

"Yes. I see that."

Port went to the door.

"If you want to start," he said, "two of them are in
the jug right now. Eighteenth precinct."

"Really?"

"Bellamy and Paternik. The charge on them won't hold
unless you get down there before morning."

"What!" His robe flapped when he rushed to the phone.
Port said, "Thanks for the ticket," but Landis didn't
hear him.

Port had let the taxi go. He walked down the street
carrying one suitcase, and Ramon had the other one.
With the dawn almost there, a clammy coldness had come
into the streets. It made the pavement look harder and the
light from the posts seemed more distant. They listened to
their footsteps and the air felt empty.

Port stopped at a corner. He put down the suitcase and
waited till Ramon had done the same.

"Where is Shelly, Ramon?"

The question didn't sound the same to Ramon as it had
before. It did not stiffen his back and make the blood
pound in his head.

"I sent her away."

If Port would hit him now, in order to force him, it
would mean little to Ramon, and the little it meant would
not have to do with Port, but with Shelly.

"How could you do it, Ramon?"

How? He thought of several answers, all true, then told
one.

"I told her you had been killed in a fight, trying to
leave."

Port sucked the cold air into his lungs, then let it come out. "Why did she leave?"

"Why stay?"

Now he would ask the next one, the one about Ramon. He would want to know why Ramon had done it. Then maybe Port would swing at him or do something like that. Ramon touched the side of his face and felt the pain. He had no more fever, just pain.

"Where is she, Ramon?"

"You are going there?"

"After you tell me."

Ramon nodded. Then he said, "Will you tell her I want to—I send my regards?"

"Yes."

Ramon turned so the street light fell on his hands, and with a small pencil he wrote an address on a matchbook cover. "She went to the West Coast. Near the Border." He gave Port the matchbook.

Port put it into his pocket. When he looked up again he saw Ramon walking down the dark street.

Port picked up his suitcases and went the other way. By the time it was full dawn he had exchanged his New York ticket for one that went the other way.

THE END
of a novel by
PETER RABE

BLACK LIZARD BOOKS

JIM THOMPSON
  - *AFTER DARK, MY SWEET* $3.95
  - *THE ALCOHOLICS* $3.95
  - *THE CRIMINAL* $3.95
  - *CROPPER'S CABIN* $3.95
  - *THE GETAWAY* $3.95
  - *THE GRIFTERS* $3.95
  - *A HELL OF A WOMAN* $3.95
  - *NOTHING MORE THAN MURDER* $3.95
  - *POP. 1280* $3.95
  - *RECOIL* $3.95
  - *SAVAGE NIGHT* $3.95
  - *A SWELL LOOKING BABE* $3.95
  - *WILD TOWN* $3.95

HARRY WHITTINGTON
  - *THE DEVIL WEARS WINGS* $3.95
  - *FIRES THAT DESTROY* $4.95
  - *FORGIVE ME, KILLER* $3.95
  - *A MOMENT TO PREY* $4.95
  - *A TICKET TO HELL* $3.95
  - *WEB OF MURDER* $3.95

CHARLES WILLEFORD
  - *THE BURNT ORANGE HERESY* $3.95
  - *COCKFIGHTER* $3.95
  - *PICK-UP* $3.95

ROBERT EDMOND ALTER
  - *CARNY KILL* $3.95
  - *SWAMP SISTER* $3.95

W.L. HEATH
  - *ILL WIND* $3.95
  - *VIOLENT SATURDAY* $3.95

PAUL CAIN
  - *FAST ONE* $3.95
  - *SEVEN SLAYERS* $3.95

FREDRIC BROWN
  - *HIS NAME WAS DEATH* $3.95
  - *THE FAR CRY* $3.95

DAVID GOODIS
  - *BLACK FRIDAY* $3.95
  - *CASSIDY'S GIRL* $3.95
  - *NIGHTFALL* $3.95
  - *SHOOT THE PIANO PLAYER* $3.95
  - *STREET OF NO RETURN* $3.95

HELEN NIELSEN
  - *DETOUR* $4.95
  - *SING ME A MURDER* $4.95

DAN J. MARLOWE
  - *THE NAME OF THE GAME IS DEATH* $4.95
  - *NEVER LIVE TWICE* $4.95
  - *STRONGARM* $4.95
  - *VENGEANCE MAN* $4.95

MURRAY SINCLAIR
  - *ONLY IN L.A.* $4.95
  - *TOUGH LUCK L.A.* $4.95

JAMES M. CAIN
  - *SINFUL WOMAN* $4.95
  - *JEALOUS WOMAN* $4.95
  - *THE ROOT OF HIS EVIL* $4.95

PETER RABE
  - *KILL THE BOSS GOODBYE* $4.95
  - *DIG MY GRAVE DEEP* $4.95
  - *THE OUT IS DEATH* $4.95

HARDCOVER ORIGINALS:
  LETHAL INJECTION by JIM NISBET $15.95
  GOODBYE L.A. by MURRAY SINCLAIR $15.95

AND OTHERS...
  - FRANCIS CARCO • *PERVERSITY* $3.95
  - BARRY GIFFORD • *PORT TROPIQUE* $3.95
  - NJAMI SIMON • *COFFIN & CO.* $3.95
  - ERIC KIGHT (RICHARD HALLAS) • *YOU PLAY THE BLACK AND THE RED COMES UP* $3.95
  - GERTRUDE STEIN • *BLOOD ON THE DINING ROOM FLOOR* $6.95
  - KENT NELSON • *THE STRAIGHT MAN* $3.50
  - JIM NISBET • *THE DAMNED DON'T DIE* $3.95
  - STEVE FISHER • *I WAKE UP SCREAMING* $4.95
  - LIONEL WHITE • *THE KILLING* $4.95
  - JOHN LUTZ • *THE TRUTH OF THE MATTER* $4.95
  - ROGER SIMON • *DEAD MEET* $4.95
  - BILL PRONZINI • *MASQUES* $4.95
  - BILL PRONZINI & BARRY MALZBERG • *THE RUNNING OF BEASTS* $4.95
  - VICTORIA NICHOLS & SUSAN THOMPSON • *SILK STALKINGS* $16.95
  - *THE BLACK LIZARD ANTHOLOGY OF CRIME FICTION* Edited by EDWARD GORMAN $8.95
  - *THE SECOND BLACK LIZARD ANTHOLOGY OF CRIME FICTION* Edited by EDWARD GORMAN $15.95

Black Lizard Books are available at most bookstores or directly from the publisher. In addition to list price, please sent $1.00/postage for the first book and $.50 for each additional book to Black Lizard Books, 833 Bancroft Way, Berkeley, CA 94710. California residents please include sales tax.